Legend *of the* Desert Bigfoot

Jake Thoene and Luke Thoene

Based on the story and characters
created by Robert Vernon
and the screenplay by Robert Vernon
and Douglas Lloyd McIntosh

Tyndale House Publishers, Inc.
WHEATON, ILLINOIS

The Last Chance Detectives and *The Last Chance Detectives* logo are trade-
marks of Focus on the Family.

Published in association with the literary agency of Alive Communications, Inc.,
1465 Kelly Johnson Blvd., Suite 320, Colorado Springs, CO 80920

Library of Congress Cataloging-in-Publication Data

Thoene, Jake.
    Legend of the desert Bigfoot / Jake Thoene and Luke Thoene.
      p.   cm. — (The Last Chance Detectives ; 2)
    "Based on the story and characters created by Robert Vernon and
the screenplay by Robert Vernon and Douglas Lloyd McIntosh."
    Summary: Four friends stuck in the town of Ambrosia, Arizona, form
a detective agency and skillfully unravel the mysterious sightings of the
desert bigfoot.
    ISBN 0-8423-2084-9 (sc)
    [1. Sasquatch—Fiction. 2. Arizona—Fiction. 3. Mystery and
detective stories.] I. Thoene, Luke. II. Title. III. Series.
PZ7.T35655Le 1996
[Fic]—dc20   95-47389

Printed in the United States of America

03   02   01   00   99   98   97   96
9   8   7   6   5   4   3   2   1

The full orb of a silvery moon glimmered above the dusty, rugged desert landscape. Swirling winds spun through the dry creek bed, whistling a ghostly tune over the entrance to an old mine. On a lonely hill above the shaft, bits of gravel scoured the dry planks of Silas Varner's shack. In a fenced yard camouflaged by tumbleweeds and pieces of junk stood an alert-looking Border collie. His ears pricked at an unfamiliar sound, and the ruff of his neck stood erect as he barked.

Sand disturbed by the tramp of heavy footsteps scraped across the flat, red paving stones that led up to the cabin door. In the moonlight, the lighter fur of the dog's shoulders stood out against his dark coat as he bristled and snarled.

Beneath the rusty tin roof, surrounded by the messy clutter of the cabin, was an old, craggy-faced man. On his hands and knees, Silas Varner, prospector and desert rat, pushed aside table and pine chairs to reveal the outline of a loose board in the floor. With the handle of a stewing spoon, he pried up the plank. Setting it aside, he stared into the hole beneath.

Sniffing, he wiped his nose on his shirtsleeve before retrieving an ironbound strongbox from the opening. On the lid, carved deep in the oak panel between the shackles, were the initials *S V.* He lifted the chest out of its hiding place and set it carefully on the floor.

The miner listened intently, hearing nothing but the howl of the wind and the barking of the dog. Silas licked his chapped lips. A bead of sweat rolled down his cheek as he extracted an iron key from his pocket and inserted it into the aging lock. It resisted at first, then opened, and Silas removed the padlock from the hasp and raised

Legend *of the*
Desert Bigfoot

the lid. Glancing furtively around him, he scooped several light gray canvas pouches from the box and dumped them onto the table.

Sifting the contents of one bag onto a sheet of tin, the eyes of the old miner sparkled like the gold dust that made a small glittering mound next to a scale and a set of brass weights. Silas grinned with deep pleasure as he adjusted the beam of the scale till it was perfectly still.

Deftly wielding a pair of tweezers despite the clumsiness of his calloused fingers, the prospector carefully moved grains of gold dust from pouch to pan balance, weighing his treasure. He added a brass weight to the right-hand pan, more gold to the left pan, then yet another weight to the right. He looked up with annoyance at the noise made by the dog, muttered to himself, then yelled for the animal to keep still. The prospector noted the weight of the gold dust, then in his cramped handwriting, patiently recorded the amount in the column of a faded green ledger.

The dog continued to bark, protesting a disturbing presence. It was anxious for the human to come out. Its warning was urgent.

"Jake!" Silas shouted again at the collie. "Pipe down out there!" But instead of subsiding, Jake's barks intensified, taking on a shrill note of panic.

The plaid-shirted miner jumped up from his

work, spilling a half-full cup of cold coffee. The bitter, dark brown fluid dribbled across the columns of weights and values, blotting the ink and angering the man. With a crash, Silas threw open the cabin door to yell into the darkness, *"Jake!* I said quiet! Don't make me come over there." The dog seemed to understand the command and was silent. The dog's owner peered around the yard but saw nothing out of place. Silas was about to reenter the shack when Jake resumed his yapping once more.

The prospector shook his head with irritation and limped out into the moonlit space. "All right," Silas announced to the collie. "Looks like you need to be taught a lesson." He continued muttering to himself as he hobbled painfully over to the collie's wire compound. As he reached the gate, Silas retrieved a leather muzzle from a post. Jake tried to slip past the man, but the miner grabbed the animal around the neck. "Hold still! Think you're smart, huh?" He slipped the muzzle over Jake's nose and buckled it in place. "Well, I'm gonna fix that." The dog's barks were reduced to anxious whines.

Silas pushed the dog away roughly. "There," he said. "That'll teach ya." At that moment there was a crash from the deep shadows beside the cabin. The miner spun around, raising his hand to shield his eyes from the glare of the cabin lights. "Who's there?" he demanded as he emerged from the dog pen. "I said, who's there?"

No answer came, except another clatter of metal. A moment later a garbage can bounced into the light, its top spinning crazily into view. Silas reached behind him and picked up a stick that was leaning against the fence. It was not a stout club, more of a walking stick really, but he brandished it like a spear, waving it in front of him. "Who's ever there better come out," he warned.

Taking a step forward, Silas was greeted by a frightening roar, and then a huge, impossibly hairy shape emerged from the dark. Startled, Silas retreated suddenly, tripped, and fell heavily to the ground. The miner clutched at his side in pain. He had just time enough to scream in terror at the approaching form before the lights and shadows danced around in front of his eyes and he blacked out.

5

2

A cloud of yellow dust chased the tow truck as it cruised along the narrow, sun-beaten desert highway. The rolling hills and the heat waves rising from the asphalt made the outline of the vehicle shimmer. Despite the heavy construction of its faded blue-and-white body, it seemed to float over the two-lane road instead of roll along it. Painted on the doors were the words *Last Chance Gas & Tow, Pop Fowler—Owner.*

The green, grassy verge that marked the edges of the roadway faded quickly into dry rocks and gravel. Mike Fowler leaned out of the open passenger-side window, thoughtfully studying the desolate scenery as the truck passed beneath the empty powder blue sky. Behind the wheel of the A-frame tow truck was Mike's grandfather, the white-haired, kindly Pop Fowler.

"Pop," Mike said, turning this attention away from the landscape.

"Yeah, Mike?"

"What do you think about Mr. Varner telling everyone that a big hairy beast knocked down his door?" Mike asked with disbelief. "He says it was Bigfoot."

Pop Fowler pursed his lips and leaned his head to one side as he continued to drive. "Any man that would run ten miles into town . . . with three cracked ribs . . . well, it sure sounds like he was in an awful hurry to get away from something."

A pair of tumbleweeds played leapfrog across the highway. A cone of dust swirling in a miniature cyclone blew particles of grit into the cab as the truck passed the mouth of an arroyo beside the road. Mike blinked, then rubbed his eyes. "So you believe him?"

Pop chuckled as he thought carefully before replying. "A bigfoot? I dunno. . . . Silas has been known to hit the bottle pretty hard. Sheriff Smitty went out there to have a look . . . didn't find any footprints. But he did say the inside of the cabin looked like it had been ransacked."

"The inside?" Mike questioned. The young man's thoughts were churning as he pondered the notion of a legendary and unproven monster showing up in the barren hills that surrounded the little community of Ambrosia. "The inside?" he repeated.

"Um-hum," Pop replied, his mind also reviewing the strange story. "And now Silas claims his stash of gold is missing."

"Wow!" Mike exclaimed. Here was a real mystery, not just the drunken ravings of an old miner. A theft was not the same as a legendary beast. Maybe there was something here for the Last Chance Detectives to explore after all. "So, is Smitty starting an investigation?"

Pop snorted. "Kinda hard when the only witness insists that the suspect is a bigfoot!" Pop peered through the glare on the sand-pitted windshield. "Say," he said, pointing ahead, "I think that's what we're looking for." Pop applied the brakes, gently slowing the tow truck as it approached their objective. A red late-model pickup had spun off the highway and was stuck in the deep sand at the shoulder of the road. Behind it, tipped over on its side, was a U-Haul trailer.

Standing beside the stranded pickup was a clean-shaven man wearing white trousers and a smooth leather jacket. His medium brown hair was thinning, and a few strands straggled across his forehead in the breeze. The man smiled and waved as the tow truck pulled alongside and stopped. Mike and his grandfather got out to approach the wreck.

"Man, am I glad to see you guys," the man said eagerly. "You must be Pop Fowler."

"Yep," Pop agreed, shaking the man's hand. "This is my grandson, Mike."

The man smiled at Pop, then nodded to Mike. "I'm Dan Plummer. Appreciate your coming out here this early."

"It's no problem," Pop said cheerfully. He motioned with his hand toward the pickup, and Plummer moved to stand between Mike and Pop as they looked at the scene, stopping beside the truck's back left bumper.

Plummer plucked nervously at the wisps of hair on his head as he began to explain. "I don't know what happened," he said, looking off down the road. "It was late. I was tired. I must have

dozed off . . . and the next thing I know . . ."
Plummer gestured feebly at the wreckage and
gave a sickly grin.

"Hum," Pop said, nodding once. "You're pretty
lucky then." Pop bent over to check for damage
to the wheels and axle of the trailer. When he
found that all was OK he said, "Well, I guess the
first thing is to get this trailer right side up."

"Right," Plummer agreed.

Pop turned to Mike. "Mike, could you go back
to the truck and get my crescent wrench from
behind the seat?"

"Sure thing, Pop," Mike replied, jogging around
to the driver's side of the tow truck. He opened the
door and tilted the blue bench seat forward. Spotting the silver-handled tool, the boy grabbed it,
returned the seat to its original position, and closed
the door.

"Here you go, Pop," Mike said, handing over
the wrench.

"Thanks," Pop replied, carrying on with his
conversation. "I thought you said you were calling me from the McAllister Place."

"That's right," Plummer replied.

"They would have let you spend the night
there, and we could have picked you up on the
way out this morning," Pop said, rubbing his
forehead.

Plummer smiled with gratitude. "Ah, well, that would've been kind, but I have a lot of expensive equipment in this trailer. I wanted to guard it."

Mike walked around to the back of the trailer, wondering what could possibly be so valuable as to keep a man out in the desert all night long.

"Why didn't you just lock it up?" Mike heard Pop ask. Of all the spooky things, to spend the night in the truck along a lonesome road in the desert.

Arriving at the trailer doors, Mike noticed that they had been bent and deformed by a tremendous force. The tops of both panels were curled outward and down as if some enormous power had been peeling a banana skin. When he took an even closer look, Mike discovered huge scratch marks on and around the doors. Excited, he called to his grandfather, "Pop, come here! Look at these doors . . . the way they're bent back!"

Pop moved rapidly toward where Mike squatted, pointing at the scrapes in the metal. Plummer followed slowly.

"And these look almost like claw marks! What could have done this, Mr. Plummer?"

Plummer stood fidgeting with his hands in his pockets. Finally he answered, "Uh, I don't know. I must have hit a rock or something when I went off the road."

Pop looked around, inspecting the roadside up and down the shoulder. The slope was dirt and gravel for hundreds of yards in both directions, and there were no obvious obstructions. "This is a sand shelf," he protested. "I don't see any rocks."

Plummer chuckled. "I just don't know, fellas. But I'll tell you one thing: If we don't get moving, I'll never make it to Albuquerque by this afternoon." He slapped the side of the capsized trailer with his hand. "Don't you think we better find out if this thing'll still roll?"

Pop was startled out of his thoughts by the sudden noise of Plummer's hand aginst the trailer and the animated tone of Plummer's words. "Right," he agreed, wrinkling his forehead. "I think the three of us should be able to get this right side up, and the hitch doesn't look too bad off. Just let me get the tow truck backed around."

Pop started the tow truck's mighty engine and pulled the machinery around so that the A-frame winch faced the side of the trailer from about ten feet away. Mike grabbed the sturdy hook that dangled from the cable and pulled out several feet of cord, dropping the slack onto the gravel. Dan Plummer watched as Mike wrapped the cable around the axle of the trailer, hooking it securely onto the frame underneath.

"All right now, Mike," Pop ordered. "You stand clear while I get this beast back on its feet."

"Sure thing, Pop," Mike agreed, retreating to the barbed-wire fence on the hillside behind the accident scene.

As Pop revved up the electric motor of the hoist, Mike curiously studied the broken and twisted strands of wire. From some of them hung long, coarse clumps of dark brown hair. Mike plucked a sample from the barbs and stuffed it in his pocket. Then, turning his attention toward the shape of the fence, he noticed that the strands had been pushed apart in a strange way: The top two were pushed upward and the bottom two downward, leaving an oval outline large enough for something big—and hairy—to have crawled through.

Pop lowered the trailer back down into an upright position. It bounced and creaked as if happy to once again be on two wheels.

"Bravo," Plummer applauded. The pickup and the trailer were reunited in no time.

Mike was thoughtful as he and Pop Fowler drove away. He patted the pocket containing the sample of hair and wondered how soon he could get together a meeting of the Last Chance Detectives. A mystery had once again come to Ambrosia!

Shining as bright as a second sun, the chrome body of the B-17 bomber glistened in the light of early afternoon. Not far from the World War II vintage aircraft being restored by Pop Fowler was the Last Chance Diner and Gas Station. Relics of Route 66, the plane, café, and pumps appeared to be deserted beside the empty stretch of highway.

But inside the retired winged creature, the Last Chance Detectives were gathered, piecing together the first clues of another case. Wanted posters, photographs of old Western movie heroes, and legendary comic books covered the curved interior walls of the plane. Spencer, the Last Chance computer whiz and electronics genius, his coffee-colored forehead wrinkled in thought, typed frantically away on his laptop computer. He was seated at the small, wooden radio-operator's table located directly aft of the cockpit. Mike and Navajo-Indian Wynona Whitefeather stood immediately behind Spence, watching as he typed. Just to the right of the table, sitting cross-legged on the floor, the fourth member of the team, Ben, slurped a soda while watching a rerun of *The Munsters* on the television.

"I'll have it up in a minute, guys," Spence promised. On the computer screen an animation box appeared. It soon filled with a frozen image labeled "Mysteries of the Animal Kingdom. The Legend of Sasquatch. 1967."

"OK, Ben," Spencer announced. "I've got it."

"All right," Ben answered, gulping down the rest of his Coke. Dropping the can, he burped, then hurried over to join the rest as the image on the screen began to flicker and come to life.

The gang watched the screen as the blurred form of a large fur-covered, man-shaped creature crossed a creek bed. "Terrific, Spence," Mike exclaimed, leaning closer. "Where'd you get this?"

Spencer moved the computer mouse, clicking an arrow at an on-screen box. The digitized film loop rewound to the beginning and the movement of the animal repeated. "I tracked it down on the Internet," Spence reported, running the loop again. "This is the famous Murphy footage of Bigfoot from 1967."

Ben, breathing heavily, squinted at the beast as he watched. "Holy cow! Look at that thing!"

"But how could there be a bigfoot around here?" Winnie argued, tossing her long, straight hair in a gesture of skepticism. "In the desert?"

Mike turned to the overall-clad girl and, raising his dark eyebrows, replied, "They've been reported all over."

Spencer froze the frame just as the animal

turned to look at the camera. The electronics expert enlarged the view, then turned in his chair. Nodding, he agreed with Mike. "In the Pacific Northwest they call him Sasquatch. Down south it's known as Mud Monster, and in parts of the Midwest they call him Old Orange Eyes. Yeti, the Abominable Snowman . . . different places, different names. Ben gazed at the screen with horrified amazement as Spencer continued. "The problem is, no one has been able to produce any real proof."

"Then what do you call this?" Ben said proudly, grabbing the sealed bag of coarse hair from Mike's hand and holding it up.

Spencer shook his head. The glow from the computer screen danced across the lenses of his eyeglasses. "All we have is some hair that we can't identify."

"Did the driver see anything?" Winnie asked Mike.

"Mr. Plummer?" Mike answered, pausing a moment to reflect. "He didn't want to talk about it. He kept changing the subject." Mike's brown eyes took on a deep, faraway look as they often did when he was pondering a problem. "But I got to thinking," he resumed. "What if he didn't really fall asleep at the wheel?"

"Huh?" Ben snorted, looking around to see where he had left his Baby Ruth candy bar.

"What if he swerved off the road to avoid hitting something?" Mike continued.

"Yeah," Winnie interjected, going along with the thought. "What if he swerved off the road to keep from hitting it, and then it attacked the trailer, like it did the old miner's shack?"

"Whoa! The bigfoot," Ben replied in an awe-struck tone. The heavyset boy abruptly threw the bag of hair into the center of the table. "But why wouldn't he just tell you the truth?"

Mike shook his head. "You saw what happened to Mr. Varner. Everyone thinks he's crazy." Mike leaned so that one hand rested on the table while he expressed his excitement with the other. "It's just possible that we have two sightings instead of one."

"But how can we prove it?" Winnie asked, biting her lip and frowning.

"I've got it!" Ben exclaimed, waving his hands to get everyone's attention.

"Oh, brother," Winnie said, flicking back her long black hair and rolling her eyes. She had heard plenty of Ben's sudden brainstorms before. They were almost always farfetched and made sense to few others besides Ben himself.

"No, really," Ben insisted as he made eye contact with each of them in turn. "Listen! All we have to do is go out to Mr. Varner's place and see if we can find any hair." Retrieving the bagful of rough strands, he concluded, "If it's a match, *bingo!*"

Mike, Winnie, and Spencer looked at each other, surprised that Ben, for once, had come up with a good idea.

"Not bad, Ben. Not bad at all," Mike complimented his friend, patting him on the back.

Winnie lifted her hands to express one final reservation. "But what if Mr. Varner doesn't want anyone poking around?"

"Oh, come on," Ben mocked, his chubby cheeks glowing with pride. "He's probably just a sweet old man."

The gang considered the proposal. Mike edged away from the table. The leader of the Last Chance Detectives knew how to get an investigation off and running. "I know," he said, capturing the group's attention. "Race you to the quads!"

The four enthusiastic sleuths scurried out the hatch in the fuselage and headed for their four-wheelers. They already felt excited, hot on the trail of their first lead in the search for Bigfoot.

3

It's up here," Mike yelled, waving to the others to pull up beside his quad runner. "Varner," he read aloud, pointing to a sagging maroon mailbox, complete with bullet holes and a crooked lid. Hanging, bent over, from a skinny post, the mailbox looked like a rag doll with a loose head. It marked the dirt road leading to Silas's house.

Winnie, in her distinctive pink helmet, soon

rolled up next to Mike, followed by Spencer. Ben lagged behind, as usual.

"Way up, eyes," Ben mumbled excitedly from behind the deep charcoal-colored visor of his helmet. "No what I aww?"

While Winnie and Mike stared with irritation, Spencer took the initiative. "Ben, sound is an acoustic energy," Spence lectured knowledgeably, "which is transferred through a medium by wave vibration."

Ben seemed confused. He cocked the knob of his still helmeted head sideways, like a large but not overly bright bird.

Spencer adjusted his body on the quad to better face Ben as he lectured. "The density of the medium and the obstacles in the path directly affect the acoustic vibrations and can inhibit a full dynamic response as well as reduce frequency range." Spence finished by lifting his eyebrows and inquiring, "Is this getting through to you?"

Ben stared, speechless, his head panning across Winnie, Spence, and Mike like the Plexiglas dome on a surveillance camera. "Whugh?"

Mike chuckled, sighed, and leaned toward Ben's helmet. With a flick of his fingers, he casually flipped open the face mask.

"I couldn't hear a word you just said," Ben complained, shaking his head.

"No kidding," Winnie replied.

Spencer looked satisfied as he lounged back comfortably on the quad and crossed his arms over his chest. "My point exactly."

"What?" Ben asked.

"Never mind, Ben," the voices of the three Last Chance Detectives chimed together.

"What did you want to tell us, anyway?" Mike asked.

Ben thought a minute, as if he had forgotten what it was he wanted to say. "Oh, uh . . . yeah. I saw Mr. Varner's mailbox up there, uh, right there," the large, curly haired boy replied, pointing.

"Is that all?" Winnie sighed. "Thank you, Ben. How could we manage without you?" she added with acid wit completely lost on Ben.

"Let's go already," Mike ordered. "The day is wasting." He throttled up the engine and pivoted his quad toward the lane leading to the miner's shack. Knobby tires sprayed a rooster tail of gravel high behind him as he raced ahead past the mailbox and up the dirt road.

"Hold it right there!" Silas Varner cried as he kicked open his front door. The splintered and weathered door clattered against the river-rock wall of the cabin. The greasy stubble that covered

23

his cheeks and the sagging bags below bloodshot eyes proclaimed that Silas was far from well.

The gang stood in stunned silence, uncertain how to proceed since Silas had not turned out to be a "sweet old man." Winnie shot Ben a hard, angry I-told-you-so look, which the hefty boy ignored with a shrug and a duck of his head.

"What do you kids want?" Silas demanded gruffly, taking another swig of caramel-colored liquid from a flat glass bottle. The prospector then let the flask dangle from a limp arm. His other hand absently rubbed his injured ribs.

Ben, Winnie, and Spencer, slightly intimidated, huddled together looking to Mike for leadership.

Accepting the responsibility, Mike turned to address the miner. "Hi. Are you Mr. Varner?"

"What's left of him," Silas said, eyeballing them suspiciously. "Do I know you kids?" He downed another swig from the bottle. The old man's mouth hung slightly open, and he panted as if he had just run up a flight of stairs.

"Um, I'm Mike Fowler," Mike replied politely. "These are my friends: Ben, Winnie, and Spence."

"Fowler," Silas croaked in a tone reminiscent of windblown gravel scraping across bare rock. "Ah yeah . . . Last Chance Gas, out on 66?"

"Yeah," Mike replied. "Pop's my grandfather."

"Uh-huh," Silas snapped, wiping his scruffy

upper lip on his brown leathery wrist. There was an uncomfortable pause and then, "Whaddya want with me?"

Mike took a step forward. "We heard," he said, pointing at the others, "about what happened last night and wondered if we could just look around."

"Yeah," Ben announced. "We're looking for hair."

Winnie shot Ben a disapproving look. Spencer dropped his head suddenly and covered the action by pretending to check his watch.

"Hair?" Silas repeated with surprise. He looked at the yard and the desert beyond as if only just then realizing that he was standing outside. Swinging his bottle as he gestured around, part of the fluid sloshed out, but the desert rat seemed not to notice or care. "Well, I seen some around by the . . ." He paused forgetfully, confused by too many different thoughts crowding into his fuddled brain. "Seein' how you're the only ones in town that believe me . . . you got five minutes."

"Did you say you know where some is?" Mike asked.

"No, I didn't," Silas yelled grumpily. "I said you got five minutes! That's all!"

Mike thanked him, and as the other three sleuths spread out in different areas of the yard, Mike stood near the fence. Winnie searched the ground around the side of the cabin, while Spencer looked inside a pieced-together plywood toolshed. Ben moved slowly around the gravel parking area, while Mike made up his mind and entered the front gate. Silas watched them intently, almost as if they were grazing chickens hunting for worms and he was seeing that they did not stray too far.

"So, you're John's boy," Silas said to Mike in a matter-of-fact voice.

Mike looked up at the porch, startled by the unexpected topic of conversation and instantly captivated by what Silas had said. "You know my dad?"

"Vic knew him," the prospector said, nodding once and pursing his lips. "Followed him around like a puppy." Then he added in a more harsh, disapproving tone, "It was always John this and John that."

"Vic is one of my dad's friends?" Mike asked in a questioning tone. "Is Vic your son or something?"

"Was," Silas answered bitterly.

"Oh," Mike replied in embarrassment. The boy's spirits, which had risen suddenly at the mention of his father, plummeted just as rapidly.

Silas leaned heavily against the pine post that supported the porch roof. "He could have stuck around here and helped me make this a good ranch," the miner grumbled. "But your old man talked him into running off and joining the service." He paused a moment to swallow the lump in his throat. "They sent him back in a casket, just like your old man."

Mike's father, an air force pilot, had disappeared on a mission during the Gulf War. His plane was known to have been shot down, but the fate of Major Fowler was unknown.

Ben broke off from his search to glare at Silas and then looked to Mike with sad eyes. Spencer peeked around the building in disbelief at what Silas had said.

"My dad's not dead," Mike argued. "He's . . . missing."

"That's not what I heard," Silas responded cruelly.

"No," Mike shook his head in denial. "They're wrong, and someday I'm gonna prove it."

The awkwardness of the moment was interrupted by a sudden shout. "Hey!" Winnie proclaimed from inside the dog pen. "I found something."

Spencer, Ben, and Mike hurried across the yard, near the enclosure where Winnie crouched.

"What is it?" Ben asked. Winnie stepped back, revealing the Border collie, Jake, lying on his side in the dirt and heat. The animal was obviously weak and helpless.

"I just found him like this," she told them.

"Hey, you kids get away from there!" Silas Varner ordered.

Mike backed away from the cage, turning to plead with the miner. "But, Mr. Varner, there's something wrong with your dog!"

"How's that?" the gravelly voiced prospector demanded.

"Well, he looks real sick or something," Ben answered.

"Leave 'im alone!" Silas said. The old man stomped down hard as he took a step off the porch. He jarred his cracked ribs and winced with the pain. "He'll be all right."

Winnie stood angrily at the door of the pen. With her fists on her hips in exasperation she shouted, "You can't mean that you're going to just leave him here like this!"

Silas bit hard on his lower lip. Aroused, he announced, "He's my dog. I can do whatever I please!"

Stunned, the gang looked at each other.

"But he's hurt! He needs to see a doctor," Winnie protested, looking down at Jake with sympathy and concern.

"Hah," Silas laughed, deliberately mocking her. "That crazy vet in town would just love to send me one of his big, fat bills."

Winnie continued trying to convince the man. "But, Mr. Varner—"

"Listen, missie," Silas retorted, "I can take

care of what's mine. You just mind your own business."

Winnie turned to Mike as he embraced the sick dog, holding it tightly to his chest. She whispered, "Mike, we can't just leave him here."

Feebly, as if trying to add his own plea for help, the dog tried to lift its head but failed.

"Oh, Mike," Winnie continued as she lovingly stroked Jake's soft fur. "Just look at him. We've gotta do something!"

Mike clamped his jaw down tight as he made his decision. He picked up the dog and carried it out of the pen toward the quad runners.

"Hey! What are you doing?" Silas cried in outrage.

Mike cleared his throat and said bravely, "I'm sorry, Mr. Varner, but your dog or not, he's going with us to see a doctor!"

"He is not," Silas screamed, moving to intercept the kids. "You put him back! Now!" The prospector coughed painfully, clutching his side, before faltering and staggering back. "Now, or I'll . . . ," Silas sputtered, unable to continue.

Mike carefully loaded the injured animal into the rack on the back of his quad.

"Can we just do this?" Spence whispered.

Winnie put her arm around Spencer's shoulders and said to reassure him, "Spence, Mike's right. We've got to take Jake to see a doctor."

Silas continued to mutter protests and half-completed threats, while Spencer, still looking uncomfortable, turned to Ben for approval. Ben plopped down on the seat of his quad and shrugged.

Silas, regaining his breath, bellowed, "You kids won't get away with this! That dog is my property. I'll call the sheriff!" The old prospector shook his fist in anger and frustration. "Do you hear me?"

Mike, Winnie, Ben, and Spence ignored Silas's warnings as they rode out. The four departing quad runners raised plumes of dust. The cloud of brown haze hung over the scene, like the gloom in the old man's mind, until long after the Last Chance Detectives and Jake the Border collie had disappeared.

4

D r. Mangus, the young, tall, dark-complected Apache veterinarian, carried Jake down a long hall past several doors on the way to the examining room. While following him, Mike could hear the barking and whining of a large number of dogs. They traveled through a hall-way lined with bookshelves, entering an open doorway at the end. Dr. Mangus lifted Jake onto the high stainless-steel examination table. He switched on a fluorescent lamp over the table and studied the cooperative collie's eyes and mouth. He took the dog's temperature and drew a syringe of blood for later study.

Meanwhile, the Last Chance Detectives studied the room and the doctor. A wall chart displayed canine anatomy, but the practiced hands of the lab-coat-clad doctor needed no reference to complete his study.

"OK, now. Hold him right there," Mangus said to Winnie, placing her hands on Jake's back, "while I get the IV." Retrieving a wheeled pipe stand with four hooks on the top, Mangus hung a fresh bag of saline solution on it, then opened the top drawer of a nearby cupboard and pulled out a fresh needle pack. Dr. Mangus was all gentle, fluid motion as he restrained Jake with nylon straps and prepared to insert the needle. He tossed the debris into a low flip-top waste can and was ready to proceed as well as to explain the procedure to the four friends.

"All right, guys," the doctor spoke in a clear and confident tone. "I'll need you to help hold him," he said as he uncapped the needle. "This may sting him a little, but he'll like the way he feels when we get the fluids back into him."

"Oh, wow," Ben whined, covering his eyes. "I can't watch this."

Mike held tight to Jake's front left paw as Mangus felt for the vein, and Spencer watched with interest.

"Here it is," the doctor spoke softly, pushing his collar-length straight hair back from his face before inserting the needle. Jake flinched slightly, raising his head to see what they had done. "There, there, boy," Mangus said in a soothing tone. "Just relax and let the IV do its job."

Jake's body relaxed, and he sank calmly down on the table, as Mangus massaged the back of the Border collie's neck and ears.

Mike asked if Jake would be all right. "So what do you think, Doc?"

"I don't see any wounds, broken bones, or obvious symptoms of disease," Mangus replied positively. "I would guess that Jake's problem is just severe dehydration."

"Ugh." Winnie sounded angry. "In other words, he hasn't been given any water!"

"Right," the vet agreed. "It's a good thing you guys brought him when you did. He's pretty far gone, but the IV and a little rest should do the trick."

Mike shook his head slowly and said, "Poor Jake."

"Old Silas used to run a pretty neat ranch—

until his son died. Then he started drinking and let things go. This isn't the first time he's been guilty of animal cruelty."

"Hmm," Spencer said, concluding some thought aloud. "Dr. Mangus, you seem to know all about animals. . . ."

"Yes," Mangus answered slowly, unsure where the question was leading. But if Spence was holding back, Ben felt no such restraint.

Ben jumped in with, "Do you really think that Mr. Varner saw Bigfoot?"

Mangus leaned back and folded his big tanned forearms just below the stethoscope slung around his neck as he considered the question. "I wouldn't rule it out," he said at last.

"You wouldn't?" Ben commented in excitement. "Not even in the desert?"

"Not at all." The vet shook his head, then raised his slender fingers to grasp his chin. "In fact, I seem to remember hearing something about an old Navajo legend. . . ."

"What does it say?" Mike asked curiously.

"I don't know," Mangus said, laughing. "I'm not Navajo. I'm Apache."

Everyone looked at Winnie as she furrowed her brows together in thought. "Wait a minute. I know it. My grandmother once told me an old legend about some kind of . . . mythical guardian

beast. . . . But do you think that could be Bigfoot?" she asked the doctor.

"A big, hairy monster on two legs? What else
fits the description?" he replied.

Winnie was still trying to remember the details
of what her grandmother had said.

"Well, come on Winnie! Don't keep us hanging," Ben demanded, poking at her back with his
thumb. "What's this about a guardian beast?"

"His name is Taquitz. Translated that means—"
she paused—"'the Guardian of the Gold.'" She continued, "The old ones believe he guards all the gold
in the Indian lands."

"And what is it old Silas has been doing all these
years?" Mangus asked pointedly.

Chills like those from a roller coaster rolled
down Mike's back. "Prospecting."

"Wait!" Ben interrupted. "You think this . . .
thing . . . is prowling around, looking for gold?"

"Who can say?" Dr. Mangus said with a shrug.
"But if there is something out there . . . Let me
put it this way: I wouldn't go camping out that
way for a while."

Three young men, friends from college, huddled
companionably around a blazing campfire. The
full moon had not yet fully risen over the mesa,

and the night outside the cheerful circle of orange firelight was dark and lonely.

A chorus of crickets resounded on the gentle breeze, an accompaniment to Sam's storytelling. Sam's hair was pulled back and concealed beneath a bandana tied at the base of his neck. It was a sensible covering against dust and the chill air, but it stretched the corners of his eyes and gave his face a gaunt, skull-like appearance. Since Sam was at his best telling creepy tales, perhaps this was the effect he intended.

Alex, the letter on his varsity jacket matching his first name, listened intently to the story, forgetting the hot dog roasting on the forked stick. The third companion, George, thrust his hands deeply into the pockets of his jacket and pulled the ball cap lower over his eyes.

"And the flames grew bigger and bigger. Like an inferno, they grew hotter and hotter, chasing him down the long corridors of creaking and moaning timber, until at last—" Sam lowered his voice, speaking softly so the others were forced to lean in to hear the words—"until he had no place to run. . . ."

George, watching with big eyes, missed his mouth with a handful of popcorn. The crickets behind them quieted as if sensing the climax.

Alex shivered as Sam continued. "And so the

townspeople had their revenge, so they thought. But at what cost? You see, when they returned to sift through the ashes . . ."

Alex nodded quickly to Sam to continue. His eyes watering from the wood smoke, his mouth open in breathless anticipation, Alex hung on every word, captivated by the story. Over Sam's shoulder he could see the outline of their tent and farther up the slope the hulking form of their parked car. The tent and the auto were somehow reassuring to look at out there in the desolate open spaces.

"No burnt clothing . . . no skeletal remains," Sam continued. "Nothing. No one really knows for sure what happened to the stranger. But some say you can still see his face—" Sam slowly reached down at his side to grasp a tin can—"in the flames of a campfire . . . like this!" he yelled suddenly, raising his voice to a shout as he threw the contents of the can into the fire. The flames erupted huge and hot.

"Aaaaaugh," Alex screamed, falling backwards, as George also scrambled away.

Sam burst into laughter. "Oh, man, did you guys jump! You shoulda seen your faces."

With tight lips Alex complained, "You didn't scare me. I was just startled."

"Yeah, right," Sam said with a mocking smile. "Then what's your hot dog doin' in the fire?"

"Oh, great! Now what am I . . . Wait, did you hear that?" Alex asked.

"What?" Sam chuckled. "I just scared you. You're not gonna get me that easy." He reached over to nudge George. "Right, Georgie Porgie?"

"No, really," Alex insisted. "I heard something, up there by the car."

George peeked out from beneath the ball cap long enough to look. "Uhhh," he moaned. "The car is moving!"

Both Sam and Alex glanced quickly around, just in time to see the car gently rocking back and forth. Frozen for a moment, they stared as the car stopped moving.

"It's just the wind," Sam said with assurance. "Man, you guys are a bunch of schoolkids."

"Oh, right, right," Alex agreed. "Prob'ly just the wind. So, Sam, hand me another one of those dogs."

"There's no more hot dogs in here," Sam answered. "Look in that bag by you."

"No, these are all gone," Alex replied, picking up the plastic wrapping and throwing it in the fire. "See? What am I supposed to eat?"

"Hey, don't sweat it," Sam told him, patting him on the back. "There's plenty more in the ice chest in the trunk of the car."

"In the trunk of the car?" Alex repeated.

"Something wrong? Think we should have brought *chicken,* Alex?" Sam said, flapping his arms. "Cluck, cluck, cluck."

"All right, already," Alex said in irritation as he stood up, still holding the empty forked stick. "I'll go get them myself."

Walking up the incline and around to the open trunk of the dented white sedan, Alex was startled to find the ice chest torn apart and the food in the trunk ravaged and scattered about. "What the . . . Hey, guys, a raccoon got into the—"

Hearing the crackling sound of brush underfoot, Alex moved softly to look over the side of the car to see what it was. By the flickering light of the dying campfire, he spotted a small patch of fur in the deep shadow beside the car. Prodding it with his hot-dog stick, it moved, then exploded into a huge, fur-covered form. "Hey! Get away," Alex screamed in horror.

"Nice try, Alex," Sam called from the fireside. "But we're not buyin' it."

Frantically trying to escape, Alex backed up in terror and stumbled into the trunk of the sedan. "Aaaaaugh!" he screamed as the car was bounced and rocked by the fury of the beast.

"Good one, Alex! But I'm still not buying it," Sam announced, unaware of what was happening.

"Look!" George shouted, pointing to the rock blocking the front wheel of their car. "It's going over!"

Alex continued to scream from the trunk as the wheel bounced free of the chock and took off like a runaway steamroller down the hill toward the tent, the fire, and George and Sam.

"Help!" Alex shouted as the sedan became airborne over a rut, crashing back down in the tumbleweeds and crushing the flimsy tent, which it then dragged along behind.

"Watch out!" Sam bellowed, diving out of the way.

His feet asleep from sitting cross-legged by the fire, George staggered across the campsite. "Whoa!" he said as he flipped over a log, barely reaching safety just as the car plowed through the fire.

Rolling down the incline, the sedan brushed against boulders, while dragging the now flaming tent behind. Finally it crashed into a ravine about fifty yards down the slope and rocked to a stop. The Levi-covered legs of the terrified Alex still protruded from the trunk.

Sam shook his head in disbelief. Without even getting to his feet he muttered, "You gotta be kidding me!"

The Last Chance Diner and Gas Station was positioned between a barren strip of Route 66 and the rugged tableland of a mesa a mile or so behind. The slope leading toward the tiny outpost of civilization was covered in rust-colored boulders that shaded drowsy lizards and pale green clumps of sagebrush.

Mike and Winnie descended the incline

toward Ambrosia with terrific speed. Their churning feet kicked up clouds of dust, and more than once only a quick jump kept a stumble from becoming a fall. The two friends tumbled down the hillside as if pursued till finally they arrived at the bottom, gasping for breath. Mike bent at the waist with his hands on his knees.

The third member of the group also obligingly stopped, then turned with a questioning look and a wag of his tail. Jake, fully recovered from his dehydration and excited at being out of the vet's kennel, wagged again and tipped his head as if to ask why the pleasant romp had been interrupted. Abruptly jumping up, the dog smacked against Mike's chest with his front paws, knocking the boy over.

"Whoa, Jake," Winnie protested. "Don't be so rough on Mike!" But her words were punctuated by her giggles.

Jake stood over the boy, covering his face with sloppy, slobbery dog kisses of gratitude and friendship.

"Ugh!" Mike spat as Jake continued to lap the boy's grimy face. "Winnie, help."

Laughing, Winnie made no hurry about pulling the enthusiastic canine away until Mike shoved the dog off his chest and tried to sit up. At last she grabbed Jake's collar and ordered him to settle down. "Come here, boy. Leave Mike alone."

Jake backed off, tail still wagging, then began lapping at Winnie's hand.

"Good boy," Mike said, getting to his feet and brushing himself off. He patted the top of Jake's head and scratched behind the shaggy ears. "Doc Mangus was right. That IV sure did the trick."

"I know," Winnie agreed, straightening the shiny braid of her long black hair. "He's so smart. How'd he know to lead us back here to the diner?"

"I don't know," Mike answered, shrugging. "Scent, I guess," he said, massaging the dog's neck. "Attaboy, Jake! Good dog! All you needed was a little help from your friends!"

As Mike and Winnie began to walk toward the café, Jake bounded ahead. "So, did your mom say you could keep him?" Winnie asked, wiping a stray wisp of hair out of her eyes.

Spotting an old can laying about twenty yards off, Mike grabbed a smooth gray stone from the ground. With a frown of concentration on his face, Mike wound up and pitched the rock. "I haven't asked her yet." A satisfying clank resounded when the lump of shale connected with the can, and Jake ran over to investigate. Smiling at his success and the dog's curiosity, Mike continued, "I mean, taking him to the vet is one thing, but keeping him . . ."

Winnie looked concerned as she said to Mike,

"You don't mean you'd actually think of taking him back to that mean old man? Mike, he almost died!"

"I just don't . . . he's not mine," Mike answered defensively, squinting one eye.

"Oh, Mike, no! There's gotta be another way," Winnie said firmly as they neared the diner, passing a pink-and-brown sign that announced "Best Milk Shakes Around."

Mike looked unhappy, then he brightened suddenly as a thought struck him. "I know," he said. "Let's give ol' Varner a call. Maybe he'll *sell* Jake!"

Winnie and Mike banged through the screen door and, passing the cash register, headed straight for the phone near the kitchen. As Winnie crossed her fingers and stood looking across the colorfully speckled countertop at the pink and blue stools of the café, Mike opened the thin phone book to the letter *V.* Following halfway down the page with his fingertip, he said, "Here it is: Varner, Silas."

Winnie laced together the fingers of both hands, placing them to her lips in hope as Mike dialed the number.

"Hello, is Mr. Varner there, please?" Mike asked politely.

"Who's this?" The harsh, grumpy voice that erupted from the earpiece was loud enough for

Winnie to hear and sharp enough to make Mike jump.

Butterflies doing loops and barrel rolls in his stomach, Mike answered, "It's Mike Fowler, sir."

"Fowler, where in tarnation is my dog?" the angry tones of Silas Varner demanded.

"That's what I wanted to talk to you about," Mike said hurriedly, rolling his eyes at Winnie. "You see, I was kind of wondering . . . well, you know . . . if you'd be interested in, um, selling him."

"Sell him?" Silas sputtered as if he was spitting out a mouthful of rock dust.

"Yes, sir," Mike agreed hopefully. "He can be a lot of trouble for you to take care of, and I thought—"

"No!" the old miner practically screamed.

Mike sighed with frustration. "Why not? He's—"

Silas cut him of bluntly. "Never should've let you on my property in the first place. Should have knowed you'd try something like stealin' my dog. Why can't you Fowlers leave me alone?"

"But—"

"I said no! And even if I was int'rested, I wouldn't sell him to no thief!"

"But we didn't steal him," Mike argued.

"Now you listen to me," Silas told Mike in a tone that allowed no further discussion. "I want that dog brought back tomorra! And that's final!" the prospector screamed as he slammed down the phone.

Mike stared at the receiver, lost in deep concern over what to do next.

Mike sadly hung up the phone and turned to Winnie with an apologetic shrug and a shake of his head.

A tear rolled down Winnie's cheek. "He can't do that," she protested, half angry and half concerned. "It's not fair. Jake'll get sick again."

As Mike sat down at the counter, a picture of dejection and worry, Winnie said she would go locate Ben and Spence to see what ideas they might have. Mike scarcely even knew when she left, nor did he notice the three young men who entered the diner to occupy a booth.

Gail, Mike's mother, had overheard Mike's end of the conversation and guessed at the rest. She left off sorting a stack of papers and receipts and sat down alongside him, putting her arm around him.

"It doesn't look like it went too well," she commented kindly, studying her son. The pale, sky blue shade of her dress matched the color of her sympathetic blue eyes.

"He says he won't sell him to me," Mike said.

The depth of his disappointment was evident in his tone.

Mike's grandmother was pouring a cup of coffee. Gail looked at the silver-haired woman before saying in a quiet but firm voice, "Then I guess you know what you have to do."

Mike swallowed hard, fighting the lump of anger that was in his throat. He shook his head violently, then said, "But I can't just take him back! It wouldn't be right."

"And it *was* right for you kids to just take him?" Gail asked pointedly.

"Well . . . yeah. It's not like we stole him."

"Then what would you call it?"

Mike sat quietly, feeling the weight of disapproval in his mother's words. Not able to answer her question, he changed his tack. "But Jake could have died if we left him there."

"So the ends justify the means," Mom stated.

Shrugging, Mike responded weakly, "Something like that."

"Mike, I know your heart's in the right place," Gail continued. "But you can't make up your own rules as you go along. The world's full of that kind of thinking . . . and it can start you down a very slippery slope."

"But, Mom, the rules weren't going to help Jake! Isn't it better for Jake to be treated right?"

"Don't mix up the two issues," she disagreed. "Nothing is right if you have to break God's rules. Mike, your dad gave you that Bible you carry around for times just like this. In Proverbs it tells us not to lean on our own understanding, but to trust in God. In other words, you do what you know is right and leave the rest up to him. It's not always easy, but that's the deal.

"Anyway, we are talking about two different things here. Maybe there wasn't time to call the authorities first, and we're all glad you saved Jake's life. But even thinking about not returning him now is different, and you know it's wrong. There are some terrific people like Sheriff Smitty and the Humane Society whose job it is to watch out for Jake now."

Mike's grandmother Kate broke in at that point. "I'm sure you already understand how to live by laws and that stealing is wrong, don't you, Mike?" Mike nodded his solemn, if still a little unwilling, agreement. "Anyway, Gail," Kate said, "if you don't skedaddle on into town, you're gonna miss that shipment of fresh vegetables."

"Oh, right. Thanks, Mom," Gail said, rumpling Mike's hair. "Gramma's right. We'll talk more later, OK?"

"Sure, Mom," Mike said, grateful that Grandma Kate had joined the discussion. He continued to study the pocket Bible given him by his father as his mother put on her sweater and prepared to leave. Mike heard the screen door open and close as his mother left, but he didn't notice that someone had sat down at the counter next to him.

"Sounds like you've got yourself quite a dilemma."

It took a moment before Mike recognized the figure as the man from the wrecked truck and U-Haul trailer. "Mr. Plummer," Mike said with surprise. "What are you doing back here?"

"I just couldn't resist coming back for some more of that small-town hospitality," Plummer said, smiling. "So who is this infamous dog abuser, anyway?"

Mike scratched his head. "Oh, an old prospector that lives outside of town. See, me and some friends were out there looking for signs of Bigfoot, when—"

"Bigfoot!" Plummer interrupted. "Out here in the desert?"

"Yeah, Bigfoot," Mike answered, sitting up excitedly. In the unhappiness over what to do about Jake, Mike had almost forgotten the mystery that had led the Last Chance Detectives to Jake in the first place. "I know it sounds strange, but Mr. Varner claims that he saw one, and well, now that you're back, I wanted to ask you if you saw anything that night that you—"

"Excuse me," another voice called from a booth behind them.

Mike and Mr. Plummer turned around to find a college-aged kid dressed in Levis and wearing a varsity jacket standing near them. His two friends were also looking on attentively from their booth.

"Did you say something about Bigfoot?" the college student asked nervously.

"Bigfoot, yeah," Plummer agreed. "Apparently my little buddy, Mike, here, has been investigating rumors around town—"

"Well, it's no rumor," the college student said. "I saw him!"

🌵

Winnie watched from under the brightly polished wing of the B-17 as a sizable crowd gathered in the sun outside the Last Chance Diner. Chattering noisily, the onlookers listened and commented as Alex and his friends made their report to a deputy sheriff about the previous night's frightening encounter. "It was enormous and hairy, and it had these huge hands! It tore up our cooler, nearly killed me when it grabbed for me like this!" Alex enthusiastically demonstrated on the deputy's arm. "And then it . . . it roared

. . . like this, *Aarrrrrggh!*" he snarled, right into the deputy's face.

Blinking and stony-faced, the deputy stepped back. "Uh-huh," he said with barely hidden sarcasm. "Do you think I should write that down?"

"Well, uh, that's what it sounded like to me," Alex answered, nodding. "Look, I know this sounds lame, but you've gotta believe us. . . . I mean, we were all there."

"That's right, officer," said Sam, slipping the dark blue bandana off of his hair. "The thing practically threw the car at us. If I hadn't jumped when I did, I wouldn't be alive to tell you this now! And then when the fire exploded—"

"Uh-huh," repeated the deputy without showing any emotion. "You sure you boys weren't . . ." The deputy pantomimed taking a drink from a bottle and got a loud howl of protest in response.

Winnie shook her head. Sighing, she turned her back on the scene at the diner and, climbing under the belly of the bomber, entered the plane through the hatch.

She had only just passed through the curtain into the detective agency headquarters when Ben leaped out at her. His arms raised like claws above his head, Ben growled at her through orange-peel monster teeth.

"Aarrgggh," Ben howled through the clenched orange rind, trying to scare her.

But Winnie, wise to Ben's pranks, did not scare easily. "See what happens when you don't floss," she remarked.

"Aw, Winnie," Ben complained, "you're no fun. Hey, I was just trying to lighten things up a bit." Ben stepped down and removed his fake fangs. "It's not like we can't have fun once in a while."

Winnie sat down at the table next to Mike. He and Spencer were examining something under a microscope. Both boys seemed preoccupied with their examination.

"What are you guys doing?"

"It's a perfect match," Spencer noted as he lifted his eye from the scope and moved the eyepiece so Mike could take a look.

"What is it?" Winnie asked.

"You know the hair I found?" Mike began.

Spencer cleared his throat and pushed his glasses back up the bridge of his nose. "Remember that hair that Mike found at Mr. Plummer's wrecked trailer, where the door was smashed?"

Winnie leaned in closer. "Yes, I remember."

Mike finished with the microscope and, sliding it over to her, said, "It's a perfect match with this other hair."

"What other hair?" Winnie questioned as she

52

rotated the focus knob until the image became clear. "Where did you find the other hair?"

"You know that college kid Alex, who says he saw Bigfoot?" Mike reminded.

She glanced up from the eyepiece of the scientific instrument and motioned for him to continue. "Right, the one outside with Deputy Sorenson."

"That's him," Mike agreed. "Well, I found more hair today on the back of his car."

"Wow," she said. "So there really is something big and gruesome out there."

"That's not all," Spencer added. "We think we know where he's going to strike next."

Ben stopped slurping the last of the orange, dropped the remains of the peel to the deck of the aircraft, and wiped his hands on the front of his red shirt. "You do?" he interrupted, walking over to the table. "I didn't hear this part. When'd you guys figure this out?"

"While you were planning how to ambush Winnie," Mike said. The leader of the Last Chance Detectives reached behind him to a small wicker magazine rack and pulled out a topographical map of the local area. "Look. Here's Mr. Varner's place," he noted, circling a tan-shaded area of the map with a fat-tipped red marker. He placed a single dot in the circle. "Right here is where he said he saw Bigfoot."

"Which was night before last," Spencer added.

Mike moved his hand slightly across the map and indicated the wavy line marking a road. "And this highway, here, is where I found the hair on Mr. Plummer's trailer." Mike added another circle and a dot.

Spencer placed his finger next to the mark on the highway and added, "Which was smashed and scratched sometime earlier."

"And here's the campsite where he scared those three guys," Mike continued, moving his hand away from the highway, past the circle on the Varner cabin, to a third location.

Spencer gave a nod and said, "Last night."

Winnie let her eyes trace the line made by the three dots together. Realizing their theory at once, she looked up with a serious expression. The barest prickle of fear made the back of her neck feel peculiar. "So . . . it's moving in *this* direction."

Spencer began to retrace the line slowly with his fingertip. "And the next human habitation in this line, the next place the creature could try to steal food, the straight path from the first three sightings is—"

"Here!" Ben exclaimed. "It's coming here!"

Mike sat back and crossed his arms thoughtfully. "It's just possible. If we're right, then we can probably expect a visit from our friend tonight."

Ben gulped hard. The swallow echoed loudly in the otherwise silent airplane. "Well, I know where I'm *not* gonna be!"

"Are you kidding?" Mike retorted. "This is our big chance." He nudged Ben's arm. "You could be famous."

"I could be *dead!* You be famous . . . or Spence . . . or . . . what's this?"

Spencer tapped his left fist with the palm of his right hand. Reaching into his grip, he pulled up four toothpicks until all stuck out evenly. "Short straw spends the night here in the B-17." Spence motioned to Ben. "Come on, Ben. We'll even let you go first."

As if his life depended on it, Ben touched a fingernail to one stick, drew back, touched another, went back to the first, then skipped one straw completely to grasp his choice and pull it out. It was really short, and Ben held his breath while waiting to see what the others drew.

Winnie scarcely looked at the three remaining options before making her selection. Ben craned his neck anxiously and groaned at the length of her straw. It was longer than his!

The next turn was Mike's, and the straw he drew was slightly shorter than Winnie's, but still longer than Ben's. The heavyset boy let out his breath with a whoosh, then took another breath and held it as Spence opened his palm to reveal the final stick.

"Let me see that, Spence," Ben whined, holding up his toothpick for comparison. "Oh, no! It isn't fair!"

6

The orange ball of the sun was just sinking into an onrushing line of heavy clouds as Ben made his way across the parking lot of the Last Chance Diner. He was headed to sentry duty aboard the B-17, and he was clearly not happy. The hefty boy kept looking over his shoulder toward the coffee shop as if hoping that someone would run after him to tell him he did not have to go through with it. "It isn't fair," he muttered to himself. "It just isn't fair."

Ben aimed a kick at a Coke can lying on the asphalt. He swung back his foot, kicked mightily at the red aluminum, and sent it skidding across the pavement. As he did this, Mike was catching up to him from the direction of the gas station.

Mike had a rolled-up sleeping bag over one shoulder. "Don't worry, Ben," Mike reassured his friend as he caught up. "I brought my sleeping bag. Jake and I will sack out on the floor. If you hear anything or get scared, we'll be there, and you can just wake me up."

Ben covered his face with both hands, still not willing to believe what he had gotten into. "It isn't fair," he repeated. "It was a setup, that's what it was!"

As they approached the B-17, they saw Spence and Winnie working outside the plane.

"C'mon, Ben," Mike encouraged his friend. "It's not that bad." Looking to his other friends, he said, "Hey, guys! Show him what you rigged up!"

"This is our low-tech alarm system," Spence said sheepishly, gesturing to a rope leading from the plane to some garbage cans. "The rope is hooked up to the garbage cans behind the diner and runs around the perimeter of the plane. The bigfoot seems to be looking for food, so he should hit the garbage cans first."

"Good thinking," Mike said, patting Spence on the back. "I went camping one time, and I remember that the garbage cans were always the first thing that bears went for."

The others crowded around to study the low-tech alarm system. Winnie smiled at Spence. "He trips the wire and rings a bell inside."

Spencer nodded, then said to Ben, "Which should, hopefully, wake you up."

"Sleep?" Ben answered, shocked that anyone could even think it was possible. "With that *thing* out there? No way!"

Winnie picked up a bundle of blankets and loaded them into Ben's arms. Spence placed a video camera on top of the pile.

"What's all this for?" Ben asked.

"Well," Spence answered, "if you *do* stay awake, we were hoping you might get that thing on tape."

"The blankets are in case you get cold," Winnie chimed in. "There's supposed to be a storm blowing in tonight."

Ben shook his head and looked up at the sky. "Perfect," he muttered.

Suddenly a trash-can lid rattled off, pulling the rope tight, and shaking the bell wildly. The four friends spun around to see what was happening. To their disappointment, it was only Mike's grandma, Kate, dumping a load of garbage.

Even though it was a false alarm, the Last Chance Detectives were pleased with the success of the system.

As they walked toward Grandma Fowler, she called out hello to them, but their responses weren't enthusiastic.

"Oh, hi, Grandma," Mike said. "It's only you, huh?"

"Only me?" she repeated. "Well, who were you expecting to take out the trash?"

"It's not that," Mike explained. "It's just that Ben and I are going to sleep out here tonight. And Spencer set up this alarm system in case the bigfoot comes around."

"Well," Kate said, smiling. "Sorry to disappoint you. I'm not hairy, I'm not eight feet tall, and I don't wear size twenty-two shoes either."

Winnie and Mike laughed, while Spencer snickered and Ben let out a loud snort.

🌵

Lightning split the black, overcast night as the first drops of rain tapped the Plexiglas bubble of the top turret on the silver B-17. The drizzle thickened at once into a downpour, filling the fuselage of the bomber with a muffled roar, like a wave breaking on a nearby shore.

Outside the plane, the water filled cracks in the dirt, softening the hardpan clay into a thick mud.

Inside the aircraft, Mike slept soundly next to Jake. The dog was breathing loudly enough for the noise to be called snoring. But Mike did not lose any sleep because of it—and neither did Ben.

Ben sat up in the watch chair, but he was sound asleep. The camera was still sitting in his lap. A small trail of drool led from Ben's mouth down to his chin.

The rope of the low-tech warning line stretched between Mike and Ben, dividing the plane in half. Since Grandma Kate, there had been nothing to disturb the bell, and it continued to remain silent.

Even though nothing seemed to have changed, Jake snorted abruptly and sat up. His shaggy ears were pricked to the alert, as if the dog sensed something was wrong or out of place. He turned his head toward the warning line and cocked it to one side as the bell rocked gently. The motion caused only a faint, slight clank of the clapper.

Jake stared down the length of the fuselage, and the hair on his neck bristled. The dog bared his upper teeth and gave a growl low in his throat. The warning line bounced again, harder this time, as Jake took a step toward the hatch.

Suddenly the bell clanked like a fire alarm, and

Jake's growls turned to barks. The alarm signal struggled and jolted on the end of the cable as if trying to tear itself loose and run away.

Startled, Mike snapped upright in the sleeping bag and looked all around the plane. He was momentarily confused about where he was and what was happening. When he realized what all the noise was about, he shouted, "Ben! Ben!"

Ben jumped in the chair as if he had received an electric shock, then rubbed his eyes with both fists.

"Ben! The bell! It's Bigfoot!"

With that, Ben was wide awake—and very frightened. Mike scrambled out of his sleeping bag to look through the side window, but the warning line pulled tight and blocked his way. The fibers of the rope creaked under the strain as something either very heavy or very strong pulled against the cable.

"Mike!" Ben shouted. The large boy fell from his chair and scrambled away toward the shelter of the back wall of the airplane. "What's happening?"

Mike whispered, staring at the taut, jerking line with wide eyes, "I think we caught something." *But I don't think we want it,* he thought.

The rope pulled against the shelves on the wall, and Jake whined a warning. The bolts creaked and moaned, and Mike thought the whole plane was going to fold in half. Suddenly the shelves ripped loose from their fastenings against the wall and came crashing down toward him. The avalanche of supplies and tools spilled electronics on the floor with a shower of sparks as the rope was torn from the wall.

"I think it got away," Ben said, petrified.

All the light inside the aircraft went out, and suddenly everything was quiet except for the constant murmur of the rain and Jake's yelping punctuated by whines and growls. "Ben! Take a look out the window," he ordered.

"Are you crazy?" Ben argued fiercely. "I'm not sticking my head up there! You look!" Another lightning bolt split the darkness in the distance, making the rain-washed sky glow all around it.

Mike crawled past Ben and put his fingers on the wall, sliding his head up slowly till just his eyes were above the window. Jake was not afraid to join him there, and both boy and dog peered into the darkness but saw nothing.

Remaining on all fours, Mike slithered cautiously toward the hatch that led to the round globe of the ball turret, which hung suspended beneath the plane.

"Mike! Where are you going?" Ben asked.

"To get a better look," Mike replied as he folded the hatch back and slid into the opening feetfirst. He put his feet on the foot pedals and turned the bubble in a slow circle toward the trash cans behind the diner.

Ben popped his head over the edge of the ball and looked down at Mike. He had been in the turret many times himself but did not think that it was the safest place to be just then. It seemed to Ben that when it came to ferocious monsters, you wanted *more* protection between you and them, not less. "Come on, Mike! This is insane! Get out of there before it's too late!"

"Just a second," Mike answered as the rotating seat came full circle. "He's got to be out there somewhere. . . ." Mike heard a heavy thud behind him, followed by splashing water. He worked to turn the machinery around again and was instantly sorry that he had not taken Ben's warning. Just outside of where Mike crouched in the turret, the huge silhouette of a hairy creature lurked. Lightning flashed behind the beast, and it stomped another claw down in a mud puddle, just a few feet away from Mike's horror-filled face. Mike screamed and stood up in the gunner's seat, nearly hitting Ben as he scrambled out of the ball and back aboard the body of the bomber.

7

The midday heat had dried all evidence of the previous night's rain. Not a cloud remained in the sky from the freakish weather that had come upon Ambrosia so quickly, bringing with it a nightmare of horror-movie proportions.

Mike, joined by Winnie and Spence, walked around the B-17 searching for evidence of the creature. Jake sensed the tension in the air as the kids examined diligently, and he joined in, sniffing the dirt around the wheels of the plane. Slowed by the muggy air and the lack of sleep after the night's excitement, Ben sat on a greasy oil drum and watched. He was mildly interested in the investigation, but the extent of his participation was to attempt a composite sketch of the nocturnal beast.

"Here! This the creature! It looked exactly like this!" Ben held up his notepad to show Mike, Spence, and Winnie his finished work. Tired of their task, they moved to Ben's side to view the masterpiece containing a large King Kong look-alike crushing a poor representation of the B-17 in one giant hand.

"Don't you think you're exaggerating? Just slightly?" Spence corrected the amateur artist.

"Hey, this thing was big! Right, Mike?" Ben turned to his friend for support. Winnie tossed her hair and returned to her previous task. Mike followed suit as Ben tagged along, still promoting his artwork.

"His feet weren't big enough to keep the rain from wiping out his footprints," suggested Spence, making a carefully calculated observation.

"I can't believe it," Winnie complained. She was tired of the argument and anxious to change the subject. "No hard evidence. No footprints. No videotape. No pictures. Nothing." She wiped the sweat from her forehead and gazed around her with disgust. Her look settled on Ben with accusation.

Ben reminded her, "We had other things on our mind, Winnie."

"Like what?" she challenged.

"Like survival." Ben grimaced as he recalled the previous night's terrifying events.

Winnie dropped her shoulders and sighed, "Come on, you guys probably scared it as much as it scared you."

Jake stopped his sniffing around, freezing so suddenly that Mike nearly walked into him. The dog barked once, turning around to see if Mike was paying attention.

"Hey, check out Jake," Mike said and knelt down next to the dog, putting a hand on his collar. Jake appeared to have found something of interest in the air near the front landing gear of the plane. "Do you smell him? Do you smell Bigfoot, boy?" The dog pulled against Mike's grip on the collar and began making anxious whining noises.

"If Jake can smell him, maybe he can lead us to him!" Winnie said excitedly over the barking.

Mike smiled and looked up at Winnie. "Yeah!" he shouted, letting go of the collar. "Come, Jake! Come on, guys. Let's get a move on! Go get him, Jake!"

Jake trotted a zigzag path away from the airplane hangar with his head stooped to the ground, sniffing deeply in the weeds around the trail. The Last Chance Detectives rode their quads a short distance behind so as not to stir up dust that might interfere with the scent.

Mike, leading the way on his dark blue quad, was armed with a long-range walkie-talkie. The radio enabled the foursome to stay in contact with Mike's mother back at their base, the diner.

Jake stopped and began sniffing around in a circle as he apparently lost the scent, and the kids came rolling to a halt behind him. "I'm not sure if this bigfoot knew exactly where he was going," Mike said as he took off his white helmet. "This path is winding all over the place, and if it goes into that—" he pointed to a large stand of cactuses in the distance—"we're not going to be able to follow on the quads."

"He was so big, Mike," Ben observed. "I don't think he could make it in there either."

"Give me a break," Winnie demanded. "Next you'll say he jumped over the Grand Canyon and disappeared."

"Actually, Ben has a point," Mike suggested. Ben beamed at the praise and stuck out his tongue at Winnie. "Thanks, Mike," he began. "You know, I—"

"Gee, wow," Winnie sneered. "First time for everything, I guess."

Ben's self-congratulation and Winnie's gibe were both cut short when Mike noticed that Jake had picked up the scent and was off and running again. The chief of the detectives immediately motored off, leaving the other three behind.

"Come on, guys," Spence said. "Let's work together. The likelihood of us solving a mystery if we can't even achieve a friendly attitude toward each other is minimal."

Winnie took off without saying another word, the bobbing of her pink helmet standing out against the darker tans and rusts of the landscape. Spence replaced his helmet and sped off next, leaving Ben behind.

"Hey, wait up," Ben called as he hurriedly lowered his visor, revved the engine, and put the quad in gear. The course of the string of four-wheelers headed right toward the cactus grove.

As they rolled up to the edge of the prickly thicket, Mike realized that Bigfoot's size had not kept him out, but was the exact quality he had used to get in, or rather, through. The succulent plants were shredded, and bits of green mushy pulp had been flung everywhere. Jake trotted right in and kept going.

"All right," Mike said, "we can't follow on the machines. Ben and I will leave our quads here and follow Jake in. Winnie, you go with Spence and try to find a way around. Hopefully you can pick us up on the other side."

"I've got a good idea," Ben said. "Why don't you go in with Jake, and I'll ride with these two and meet you."

"Are you chicken, Ben?" Winnie snapped.

"Stop fighting!" Spence yelled. "Didn't you hear a word I said back there?"

Mike stepped back in surprise at the outburst from this normally quiet boy.

Spence glared at Winnie. "We're not going to find Sasquatch, Bigfoot, or anything if you don't desist from this childish name-calling. And you, Ben, stop arguing and do what Mike says. Come on, Winnie, let's go." The pair motored off to the north to look for a path around the dense, thorny plants.

"Wow!" Mike said as he made his way between the plants that were still standing.

"I didn't think Spence had it in him."

"Yeah, a real motivator," Ben said sarcastically.

The boys continued walking through the cactuses, following loosely behind Jake. After ten minutes, they hadn't come across anything other than trampled vegetation.

"You know, Ben," Mike suggested, breaking the quiet that had settled over them, "it's all right to be afraid now and then, but this thing probably isn't a monster at all."

"Ha-ha," Ben said without humor. "If that's a joke, it's not very funny. You saw it outside the plane! Of all people, I'd think you would be the one to worry as much as me."

Mike thought about that as he looked for Jake, who was barking somewhere in the middle of the tangled mess of toppled cactus. "I guess I'm just trying to say Winnie's right about this thing being scared, too. Look how it came in for food and then took off out here in the desert."

There was a rustle from the nearby brush. At first Mike thought it was Jake, but then he heard the dog barking farther in the distance. Something rattled the undergrowth again, and whatever it was, it was close by.

"Mike?" Ben squeaked. He, too, had heard the scratching and now noticed breathing noises that were not his own apprehensive pants. "Mike?" he repeated more urgently.

Mike shushed Ben and bent down near ground level to peer through a gap in the cactus trunks. There in the shadows shone a pair of grayish yellow eyes, and the panting was replaced by a low growl.

Unhurriedly, Mike stood up again and held his finger to his lips to warn Ben to keep quiet. Then he led the way across the remaining thicket to Jake.

It was just a few minutes till he reached the dog, then sat down and petted him. Ben stumbled out behind him and nearly fell over them while looking over his shoulder.

"Mike," he pleaded, "don't stop! We gotta get away from Bigfoot!"

"Bigfoot," Mike laughed. "Ben, that wasn't a bigfoot."

"Oh, no?"

"No," Mike said, pointing to the path behind them where a low, lean form with a gray bushy tail trotted away. "It was a coyote."

8

J ake trotted to the top of a hill, sniffing the
air and looking into the distance. The mid-
afternoon sun beat down on his back, and
he panted to keep cool. Mike had brought
some water and a dish for him, but even
after the incident in the cactus patch, Jake did
not seem to want to stop long enough to drink.
He had pestered Winnie and Spence and had
walked around in circles nervously during the

time it took Mike and Ben to retrieve their quads. The Last Chance Detectives could sense his enthusiasm for the search.

The quad runners crested the rise, and the four friends stopped to survey the landscape before following the dog down the other side. "Wow!" Ben exhaled in a drawn-out exclamation of approval. "That dog's got to be part bloodhound!"

Jake had led the sleuths straight to the rusted, hulking machinery of an abandoned rock quarry. Back in its operating days, this was the spot where ore mined in the surrounding mountains was trucked to be crushed and refined.

"Better do a radio check," Mike observed as he reached into the crate strapped to his vehicle and retrieved the walkie-talkie. "Mother Hen . . . this is Desert Eagle," he called, using their call signs. "Do you read me, Mother Hen? Over."

Back at the diner, Mike's mom, Gail, smiled when she heard the incoming signal. She set the coffeepot down near the matching walkie-talkie to answer the call. She tried to reply in an official-sounding, serious voice, but her tone was unnaturally deep, and she held back a laugh with difficulty. "Mother Hen to Desert Eagle, reading you loud and clear. Can you report your current coordinates?"

The detectives chuckled at her teasing. "OK,

Mom, cut it out. We're out at the old rock quarry."

Spence pointed to the rock-crushing equipment and explained to Winnie how the chemical processes in the settling tanks depended on the solid rocks being ground into particles as fine as coffee. Winnie nodded her understanding.

Ben waved at the maze of conveyor belts and gravel chutes and commented that it looked like the demented roller coaster from the sci-fi film *Zombies in the Fun House.*

Jake began yapping again as he ran ahead of the group down the slope. He was headed toward the large shop building, made of corrugated steel and plywood. "I think Jake's on to something," Mike continued to his mother by radio. "He's barking like crazy."

"Is everything OK?" Even through the static of the intervening airwaves, the concern in Gail's voice could be heard.

"Yeah, we're fine," Mike reassured her. "But by the way Jake's acting, I think we're getting close."

"Well, you kids be careful." Gail's voice crackled out of the handheld speaker, this time in her normal tone. "I don't want you walking into a cougar's den or something."

"Don't worry, Mother Hen. We won't take any unnecessary risks. Over and out."

When Mike released the transmit button, Ben said, "What are you talking about? This whole case is an unnecessary risk."

Ignoring Ben's comment, Mike glanced toward Jake, who was now yelping frantically at the large side door of the building. "What's with Jake?"

"He's focused like a laser on the largest structure," Spence said as he peered through his binoculars.

Jake was scratching on the panel as though the trail he had been following led directly into the derelict building.

"C'mon," Mike said. "We'd better get down there." He fired up his quad and led the way down to the quarry.

Outside the rusted hulk of the abandoned construction were piles of discarded and broken equipment. From the top of the ridge the structure had looked small, innocent, and harmless in the bright light of day. But up close it took on a more sinister, dangerous appearance as twisted pieces of metal and the abandoned jaws of earth-moving machinery seemed to grow in size until they towered over the detectives' heads.

The four friends hopped off their quads right in front of the large warehouse door and looked around for Jake. The dog had disappeared.

"He must have nosed open the entry and run in," Mike suggested.

"Better him than us," Ben said.

Spence was searching the ground for evidence of the trail that Jake had followed. "Look!" he shouted, pointing to a large indentation in the dust. "What are these footprints?" There, just in front of the door, was an enormous paw print big enough that all of Jake's prancing in front of the entrance still had not covered it. "I would estimate that it is ten times the size of the dog's footprint," Spence concluded.

Winnie took a look and said, "That's no bear. And that's no cougar either."

"Bigfoot!" Ben shouted. He took a step back from the door, which a gust of wind chose to push slightly open at that moment.

Jake's muffled barking could be heard coming from inside the building. "Jake!" Mike yelled. "Here, boy! Come back!" Mike started in to retrieve him.

Spence grabbed Mike's arm. "Wait a minute. It might not be wise to rush in. Maybe we should wait out here and let that thing come to *us*."

"Right!" Ben agreed. "No unnecessary risks. Remember?"

Mike protested, "But Jake's in there! I can't let anything happen to him."

"If one of us goes in," Winnie stated firmly, "we all go. There's safety in numbers."

"No, I think one person should stay here," Ben protested.

Winnie glared at him.

Ben noticed her stare. "To call for help!" he added defensively.

Winnie had an acid-tipped comment ready to launch when Mike unexpectedly said, "You're right, Ben." Mike unclipped the walkie-talkie from his belt.

Ben smiled briefly when he thought he was the one elected to stay outside, but Mike passed the radio to Spence.

"Here," Mike said. "You're our communications whiz. Call Mom and tell her what's up."

Ben went pale, but the no-nonsense look on Winnie's face warned him not to argue.

Pushing their way through the old, broken-down door, Mike, Winnie, and Ben stepped carefully into the musty building. The dust they stirred up filled the light rays darting in through various holes in the roof. The stale air reminded Ben of dead things, and he gulped loud enough for Winnie to turn and shush him.

🌵

Back at the diner, business was really picking up. It was the middle of the week, and eighteen-wheelers laden with all kinds of goods were passing through Ambrosia constantly. Most stopped at the Last Chance Diner to get a bite to eat before continuing their trek through the barren desert.

Inside the fifties-style vintage café, country music played on the jukebox only to be drowned out by fifty different conversations about what cargo was going where. Mike's Grandma Kate was busily taking orders from and cleaning up after the hungry drivers while Gail supervised the kitchen.

The cook was hastily preparing meals for the hungry truckers, putting plate after plate on the counter to be served. As he did so, the walkie-talkie, perched just on the other side of the window, was bumped. It wobbled feebly on the edge of the counter as if trying to keep its balance, spun round once, then tumbled into the tub of sudsy water with a gurgle and a fizz.

At that exact moment, Spence was trying to carry out his duty as radio officer. "Mother Hen?" he said into the microphone of the walkie-talkie. "This is Desert Eagle. Do you copy?" When there was no answer, he tried again, and then a third time. Confused, he looked the radio over to see if there was any damage that could have caused the malfunction. Seeing none, he tried again. "Mother Hen, come in, please! Desert Eagle really needs to talk. Mrs. Fowler, are you there?" Spence released the transmit button. *Why doesn't she answer?* he asked himself.

🌵

Inside the abandoned building, the beam of Mike's flashlight illuminated a corridor of packing crates, overturned boxes, and nameless junk that might once have been valuable equipment. He walked forward boldly, forcing himself to keep moving.

Ben and Winnie thought Mike was really brave, but actually he felt the same thing they did—a sinking sensation that something very scary was lurking in the dark corners of the room. *Don't look back,* he told himself. *Just concentrate on what you're in here for.*

"Jake!" Mike called through an unpleasantly scratchy throat. "Here, boy!"

Ben tried to join in with a whistle, but found he was breathing too hard and could not make his lips form anything other than a useless whooshing.

Hoping to see more of the room, Mike asked, "Ben, do you have an extra flashlight in your pack?"

"Nope," Ben answered. "There wasn't room."

"Well," Winnie quizzed, "what *do* you have in there?"

"Important stuff . . . stuff to eat." Ben slung the pack down to one arm and unzipped it partway. "In case we get hungry."

Winnie rolled her eyes and looked around the dim outline of the warehouse, letting her eyes adjust to the pale light that seeped in from outdoors. "Jake isn't barking anymore, is he?" she asked.

"OK, everybody quiet and listen," Mike ordered.

Ben had to clamp both hands over his mouth, but soon the echo of two barks could be heard.

"That's Jake," Mike said. "Come on." The tall, lean leader of the group found a passage from one part of the structure into another. The three were soon surrounded by even taller piles of junk and crates covered in canvas and dripping with cobwebs.

"Wow," Winnie said, gazing around them. "Look at the size of this place."

Mike concentrated on the search for the missing canine. "Jake! Where are you, boy?" he called again, but it was entirely still once more.

Ben was starting to relax in the better light that came from large holes in the ceiling when the stillness was shattered by a large crash! It sounded like a giant had torn open part of the roof and thrown the corrugated metal down onto the concrete floor. Everyone froze in their tracks.

"What was that?" Mike whispered.

Winnie gave Ben a look that asked, *What did you do this time?* but Ben was staring at Mike.

"I've got a bad feeling about this," Ben whimpered. "Don't you think we oughta—"

"Shhh," Mike scolded. "Listen!" A scraping noise could be heard coming from the direction of the thunderous clatter. It sounded like feet scuffing along the ground. Then a low growl echoed through the room.

"That doesn't sound like Jake!" Winnie pointed out, giving voice to what Ben and Mike also thought but were afraid to say.

"No," Ben agreed. "It's much bigger!"

"Nobody panic," Mike urged. Then listening again, he added, "But I think it's coming our way!"

"Run!" Ben yelped. The group took off running straight ahead, hoping to put some distance between themselves and the monster. Then they realized that the shuffling footsteps were ahead of them. They turned, set off down a side alley, ran a few short steps, and bumped headlong into a dead end, blocked by a wall of crates and barrels ten feet high. They crisscrossed the aisle, looking for a way through the maze of boxes, but found none.

Mike pulled up the corner of a tarp that covered an empty crate turned on its side. "Quick! Everybody under here!"

Winnie scooted into the shelter with Ben close behind. Mike took a last look around, then ducked into the crate, pulling the tarp down behind him. There, quiet as church mice, they huddled, hoping the lurking creature would pass them by.

At the Last Chance Diner, the afternoon rush had just ended, and things were finally quiet enough for Gail to wipe her forehead and breathe a sigh of relief. As she did so, it occurred to her that she had not heard from the desert-exploration team in quite some time. With no real worry yet, but a nagging sense of something out of place, she went in search of the radio. It was not where she had last seen it.

"Mom?" Gail called to Grandma Fowler. "Have you seen the walkie-talkie?" She walked around the kitchen a second time.

"Why, no, dear," Grandma Kate replied, joining in the quest. "The last place I saw it was right in the order window above the . . ." She trailed off, her eyes catching a faint glimmer of the walkie-talkie's gray outline below the surface of the dirty dishwater.

When she fished it out, suds dripped from every opening. It was clear without even bothering to test it that the radio was ruined.

"I'd better call Sheriff Smitty," Mike's mom said, walking to the phone. "I'll see if he can run out there and check on them for me."

A shadow fell over the outside of the tarp that covered the hiding place of the three Last Chance Detectives. Ben's teeth chattered, and his head, which was leaning back against the crate, rattled the wood. Mike grabbed his arm to steady him. Ben squeezed his eyes shut, as if when he could not see danger, it did not exist. "Oh, please, oh, please . . . please . . . ," Ben whimpered over and over.

Suddenly the edge of the tarp lifted, and a snout poked under. The nose was followed an instant later by a pair of bright eyes and a shaggy head. It was Jake.

"Jake!" Mike exclaimed with relief. "It's only you. Come here, boy!" Mike held up the tarp for him to enter, but the dog's ears pricked up and he glanced around. "What's the matter, boy?" Mike asked, suddenly uneasy again.

Jake's ruff bristled, and he growled at something out of sight from Mike's position. The dog backed out a few steps, then turned and fled, leaving the young detectives to face whatever was coming.

Another, much larger animal could be heard sniffing around the hiding place. The unseen menace shuffled around the concrete floor, then moved away from the trio's place of concealment.

"Whew," Ben sighed. "That was a close one. For a minute there I thought he had us!"

Suddenly a huge, muscular, and very hairy arm ripped through the far side of the tarp, groping around for the occupants!

Ben dodged out of the way and huddled against Mike and Winnie as they struggled to avoid the grasp of the monster. They held their breath in fear! There seemed nowhere left to get away from it. Then, in answer to the group's silent prayers, the arm was withdrawn.

Just as they relaxed, hoping that the creature would not come again, the entire tarp was ripped from its resting place on the crate. *"Aaaagh!"* the three shrieked in unison.

The beast joined in with a huge bellow that made Ben scream even louder. Mike rapped his flashlight against his palm to turn it on. When it came on, the beam caught the creature directly in the face, causing it to jump back and cover its eyes.

It took Mike a couple of seconds to retrain the light on the monster. When he did, he couldn't believe his eyes! "You're not going to believe this," he told the others, who were still shielding their faces from the danger. "It's only . . . a . . ."

Winnie turned and then wrinkled her nose in confusion. "A gorilla?"

Ben finally looked and asked, "A gorilla?"

"Yeah," Mike said. "And he's eating your candy bar."

The gorilla had drawn back, sat on its haunches, and was munching on a candy bar that had fallen out of Ben's pack.

When he finished it, he advanced on the detectives once again, a deep growl punctuating his hunger.

They panicked again. Thinking quickly, Mike asked Ben, "You got any more candy in there?"

"Sure!" Ben said quickly, pulling out a whole stack of the hot, sticky chocolate bars.

Mike took one and held it out for the gorilla. The three friends watched in amazement as the animal took it from Mike's hand, almost smiled, then started to unwrap the bar. The three friends looked on with awe.

"He seems almost friendly," Mike noted.

With a smile, Winnie added, "And hungry, too."

Ben, for the first time since the adventure began, wasn't afraid anymore. He finally smiled and said, "Wait till Spence gets a load of this!"

9

Spence's heels dug twin furrows in the ground in front of him as he was forcibly moved closer to the gorilla. Having easily lured the ape outside the quarry building with another piece of candy, Mike and Ben were finding it much harder to coax Spence any nearer at all.

"Go on, Spence," Mike urged. "It's OK!"

"Yeah," Ben added, now anxious to show off his courage, "he's not vicious or anything."

Ben thrust a candy bar into Spence's fist and then forced the boy's hand forward by pushing on his elbow with both hands. Spence's eyes widened as the gorilla looked up and stretched out a thick arm covered in long, dark brown fur.

"Go on," Ben prodded. "He's waiting for you."

Spence stretched the hand holding the chocolate to the farthest reach of his fingertips and leaned until he was as far forward as he could manage without falling over. As if mimicking his behavior, the ape also extended only two fingers and gingerly took the tip of the candy wrapper before gravely drawing it back and opening it.

"Wow!" Spencer exclaimed. "But . . . where did he come from? This is no bigfoot, but the arid terrain of the desert is not the usual habitat for gorillas either."

Mike shrugged. "I don't know. Maybe he escaped from a circus or something. He seems tame enough, like he's used to being around people."

Back at the quad runners, Jake, tied by his leash to Mike's machine, kept up a running monologue of barks, yips, yelps, and other signs of warning and unhappiness. "Jake's sure not used to him yet," Winnie observed.

"Oh, wow!" Ben announced in his listen-to-this-great-idea voice. The tone made Winnie roll her eyes even before she heard what he had to say.

"I wonder if our folks will let us keep him. . . . I mean, talk about a great mascot!"

Winnie just shook her head. There was no point in saying anything; Ben was just Ben. The girl turned her face away from the scene and by doing so caught sight of some movement over by the derelict conveyor hoists. "Guys!" she said. "We've got company."

Through the haze and dust they could see a man dressed in a blue, fleece-lined jacket, walking toward them. Mike thought at once that he looked familiar, and as the figure came closer, Mike said, "It's Dan Plummer. Hey, Mr. Plummer," he called, waving his arms.

At that moment Plummer pulled a shotgun into view from where he had carried it in concealment by his side. Winnie was the first to give the alarm: "Mike, he's got a gun!"

Mike spotted the weapon also. "Hey!" he yelled. "Hold on!"

Plummer brought the shotgun up to shoulder level, aiming it straight at the gorilla. "You kids get out of the way!" he ordered roughly.

Instead of obeying, the four friends ran toward him. "Wait! Please!" Winnie shouted.

"It's OK, Mr. Plummer!" Mike pleaded. "He's gentle!"

There was a roar and a puff of smoke from the

gun's muzzle. The ape flinched and grabbed his side in obvious pain, then toppled over onto his side in the dirt.

"You killed him in cold blood!" Winnie accused as Plummer walked between the astounded Last Chance Detectives. "You're as bad as a murderer!"

Plummer bent over the body of the ape. "He's not dead," he said calmly, reaching into the thickly matted fur and withdrawing a small, red-feathered dart from the beast's hide.

"A tranquilizer dart?" Winnie exclaimed.

Plummer nodded and pocketed the barb. "Eight cc's of Thoralen. He should be out for a while. But don't worry, he'll be fine."

Though reassured that the gorilla had not been harmed, Mike knew that a lot needed explaining here. *Why did this man show up here and now with exactly the right weapon to subdue a jungle animal?* "Mr. Plummer," Mike said firmly, "what's going on?"

Plummer grimaced as he stood and rubbed his hands against the legs of his jeans. "Mike, I owe you an apology," he said with evident sincerity. "The other day I wasn't exactly honest with you and your grandpa."

"What d'ya mean?" Mike demanded.

Holding up his hands as if to ward off Mike's suspicions, Plummer continued, "Oh, it's true, I did fall asleep at the wheel. But those scratch marks and the hair you found, they were made by this big fella when he got away from me after the accident. I've been tracking him ever since but wasn't having much luck until I saw your dog got on his trail."

Winnie let her eyes roam back to the tracks made by the quads as they pulled up at the quarry and then thought about the direction from which Plummer had appeared. "You followed us!"

Plummer nodded with a sheepish grin.

"But why didn't you just tell us the truth?" Mike demanded.

Plummer looked embarrassed. "I couldn't exactly. See, if the authorities knew that I had him, I could be in some very serious trouble. That's why I need your kids' help."

Ben folded his arms across his chest with suspicion. "What kind of help?"

Pointing at the ape, Plummer explained, "We need to keep our gorilla friend here a secret. Just between us."

Winnie was not sympathetic. "He doesn't belong to you, does he?"

The tone Mr. Plummer took was soothing and pleasant. "I don't think a beautiful animal like this can really belong to anybody. That's why I liberated him, so he could be released back into his natural habitat." The man looked from face to face, reading what impression he was making on each of the detectives.

"Liberated?" Spence quizzed. "From where?"

Now his manner changed to one of an adult dealing with kids. "Look," Plummer urged, "the less you know, the better. But trust me when I say that the previous owners were only concerned with making a profit. He," Plummer paused to wave gently at the sleeping gorilla, "was living under such inhumane conditions—he wouldn't have lasted another year."

"But a gorilla like this has got to be worth thousands," Mike pointed out, remembering the discussion with his mother. "Was it right to just take him?"

Now Plummer sounded stern. "The question is, Would it have been right to just leave him there? Think about it, Mike. It's the same thing you guys did for Jake, and for just as good a reason. If you stop and think about it, I think you'll realize that we're on the same team!" Plummer again scanned the group. "So . . . can I count on you guys?"

There was a long silence. Mike looked from Jake to the gorilla and then back to Plummer's smiling, expectant face. "Yeah, I guess so," he said.

Plummer looked relieved. "Good! I knew you kids were—" Plummer interrupted himself as he saw a vehicle approaching. "Hey!" he said abruptly. "Who's that?"

Spence peered at the advancing gold pickup and replied, "It's Sheriff Smitty."

"The sheriff!"

"It's OK," Ben said. "He's our friend!"

Plummer ignored the reassuring words and instead rushed toward the gorilla, which he covered with a tattered discarded canvas. While arranging this screen, he was giving orders. "You kids gotta cover for me! I'm sure he's a swell guy, but if he finds me with a stolen gorilla . . ." Plummer ducked inside the warehouse and pulled the door closed. As he did so he added, "Mike, listen. That gorilla—his life is in your hands. . . . Understand?"

The line of kids stood in confused silence as Sheriff Smitty's truck roared up to the scene. "So, um, guys," Mike said out of the corner of his mouth. "What do you guys think?"

Winnie was wavering. "It's not like Mr. Plummer's an escaped convict."

"He *seems* OK," Spence added.

Ben only shrugged and looked at Mike for leadership.

"Then it's agreed," Mike said with more assurance than he felt. "We hold off telling . . . for now, until we can think things over."

By now the sheriff's pickup had rolled to a

stop. Smitty got out, wearing his cowboy hat and sunglasses, and walked toward the group. "What's going on here?" he said cheerfully.

"Nothing much, Sheriff," Mike mumbled.

"Your mom got worried, Mike," Smitty explained. "She asked me to come out here and take a look."

"Oh, ah, no problems here," Ben chattered, spreading his hands wide.

"Nope," Winnie added.

"Everything's under control," Mike concluded.

The officer squinted at the Last Chance Detectives and wiped his forehead. "You all are acting kind of funny. You sure nothing's wrong?"

"Positive," Ben agreed. "Have a look around for yourself."

Winnie shot Ben a how-could-you-say-that look.

Smitty scratched his head. "Well, I suppose—" Suddenly he stopped, removed his sunglasses, and focused on some movement behind the kids.

Despite the heavy sedation of the tranquilizer, the gorilla grunted and rolled over beneath the tarp, pulling the canvas off of his hairy body.

In shocked surprise, the sheriff drew his gun and stumbled back a step. "What in blue blazes? You kids, get back!"

For the second time in ten minutes, the four

friends found themselves defending the gorilla. They ran in front of the ape and knelt down, blocking Smitty's shot. "No, no, Sheriff!"

"No, Sheriff Smitty! Don't shoot!"

"He's tranquilized!"

Smitty ordered, "You heard what I said! Get behind me . . . now!"

"But . . . ," Mike protested. Then he had another shock: Plummer was sneaking up behind the sheriff with his shotgun. Mike's protest to Smitty changed to a warning shout. *"Noooo!"* But it was too late as Plummer swung the butt of the shotgun, cracking Sheriff Smitty in the back of the skull, dropping him to the ground.

Winnie was the first to recover from her surpise. She ran to Smitty, followed by the rest of the kids. They looked at Smitty with concern and cast accusing glares at Plummer.

Plummer picked up Smitty's gun, a guilty expression on his face. "Well, why are you looking at me like that?" he demanded. "You saw what happened. I had no choice! He could have shot the gorilla." He emptied the handgun and threw it in the brush.

"He was trying to protect us!" Winnie exploded.

Plummer was through arguing with a bunch of kids. "I don't have time for this. I've gotta get my trailer. You kids stay put." And the blue-jacketed man ran off to retrieve his pickup truck and trailer.

"Oh, Smitty," Winnie sniffed. "I'm so sorry."

"Is he gonna be OK?" Ben asked anxiously.

"I don't know," Winnie answered in an angry voice.

"Man, how'd we ever get ourselves into a mess like this?" Ben moaned.

"Mike, what are we gonna do?" Winnie asked. Everyone looked to Mike for a response.

"We're gonna do what we should have done in the first place," he said firmly. "What we knew right from the start."

truck and trailer.

10

D an Plummer wheeled his pickup truck
and trailer around in a dusty circle,
stopping so that the rear of the trailer
was near the sleeping gorilla. Plum-
mer got out, trying once again to act nice and win
back the sympathy of the Last Chance Detectives.

But the kids didn't buy it. Steely eyed, all wore
faces harder than the boulders ringing the old
quarry. Mike stared at Smitty's attacker without try-

ing to hide his animosity or his resolve. Winnie still bent over the sheriff with Ben standing nearby.

Plummer remarked in a forced, put-on friendly way, "Mike, do you think you could give me a hand loading him into the trailer?" He set about opening the trailer doors and paid no attention when Spence went around the side of the rig.

"I'm sorry, Mr. Plummer, but we can't let you leave."

Plummer gave a barking laugh of disbelief. "What? You're kidding, right?"

Backed up by the others, who nodded their agreement, Mike continued, "It's over. We can't go along with this any longer."

The creaking of the pickup's door called Plummer away from an angry response. He turned in time to see Spencer emerge from the cab of the truck, ignition key in hand. "Aw, c'mon," Plummer coaxed. "Gimme the keys, OK? Just gimme the keys."

As the man started toward Spence, the boy tossed the key ring in a perfect arc over Plummer's head. Mike grabbed the keys on their descent and called sharply to Ben, "Ben! Come here!"

Plummer sidled toward Mike, not menacing exactly, but closing in. His voice still had a wheedling tone. "Mike," he said, "I'm serious. . . . Hand 'em over, buddy."

"Ben," Mike instructed sharply as he eyed Plummer's advance. "Go to Smitty's truck. Radio Arlene. Tell her to send a deputy."

That command shook Plummer out of acting the good-natured friend. *"Hold on, Ben!"* Plummer roared, stopping Ben in his tracks. "Now, before you kids make a rash decision, you better make sure this is the way you want to do this." None of the four friends missed the threat in his tone. Spence, Winnie, and Ben looked at Mike for a decision.

"Go on, Ben," Mike said firmly and calmly.

Ben opened the door to the pickup and sat inside the vehicle, ready to call Arlene. Plummer rushed to Smitty's truck and wrenched open the door. An instant later the microphone of the radio was ripped from Ben's hands. Plummer ripped the cord from the dashboard and threw the mike into the surrounding weeds.

He glared at the kids and demanded, "Now! About my keys!"

Mike spotted the evil intent in Plummer's eyes and whirled away and ran with Ben's words "Run, Mike, run!" ringing in his ears.

Sprinting along the side of the quarry buildings, Mike looked for an opening to duck into but found none. There was an acre of open ground in front of him, and Mike was afraid the man's longer legs would catch him. Then he spotted the ladders, ramps, and girders of the abandoned ore conveyors and swerved sharply toward them.

Plummer was only twenty feet behind Mike and rapidly closing the gap when Mike jumped upward onto the rungs of the ladder and began to climb.

"Quick!" Winnie urged. "We've gotta do something!"

"Yeah, but what?" Ben groaned. He could not tear his eyes away from the chase. Mike had reached a catwalk and was dashing across from one rusted steel tower to another just as Plummer reached the top of the ladder.

"Winnie," Spence commanded, breaking through the indecision. "See if you can find the microphone and fix Smitty's radio! Ben, come with me. I've got an idea."

Like the ruins of an ancient carnival ride, the framework of the rock-crushing equipment was a tangled mess of sweeping conveyor belts, chutes with vertical drops, and swaying supports at dizzying heights. Mike crossed another catwalk. The bottom rungs of the next ladder were broken out, cutting off his escape in that direction.

With Plummer pounding across the rattling boards of the walkway, Mike changed plans and

jumped onto the inclined surface of a conveyor
belt. Feet slipping under him, he scooted upward
once more.

🌵

Spence yanked open the door of Plummer's truck.
Ben shuddered as he watched the chase and urged,
"Hurry, Spence! Hurry!"

The smaller boy tossed aside some rags and a
shirt on the floor of the truck. His flurry uncovered
a small metal box, which he instantly handed to
Ben. He also pulled out a silver toolbox.

Opening the metal box, Ben said, "Look at
that! It's gold!"

Spence ignored the distraction of the precious
metal and searched through the toolbox. "Forget
it!" he said. "This is what we're after!" He held up
a small, green plastic case.

"What is it?" Ben wanted to know.

"Tranquilizer darts."

🌵

Mike struggled up the belt with Plummer now
following him up the slippery incline. Mike scam-
pered up a few feet before getting tripped up.
Plummer lunged, grabbing at Mike's heels. Mike
kicked free and scrambled up the belt again with
Plummer close behind.

At the end of the belt, Mike sprinted up another catwalk to the top of a platform.

A sheer drop of eighty feet confronted the boy. There was nowhere to go! Plummer was smiling again, knowing that he had Mike trapped. "Looks like this is the end of the line," he puffed. "You're not going anywhere!"

Overhead a power line was suspended from the very top post of the steel girder. Mike's eyes traced the curve of the wire as it drooped downward to intersect another part of the machinery. It was a desperate gamble, but there was no time remaining.

Just as Plummer lurched toward Mike from behind, the boy grabbed a castoff piece of conveyor-belt fabric. Flipping the strip of rubber over the cable, Mike grabbed it with both hands and flung himself off into space.

There was a terrifying second when Mike felt the wire give under his weight. He thought the attachments would not support his weight and the power line would drop him to the packed earth far below.

But by the time the frightening idea had surfaced in his mind, the ride ended with a crash. Mike's feet plowed into a barricade of boards on the other tower. The timbers were rotten with age, and he plowed through them to land in a heap on the grid of a platform. Hurriedly, he looked back up the wire to see if Plummer would try to repeat the wild flight, but the man had disappeared.

Looking down over the edge, Mike caught sight of his friends. "Ben, Spence," he called, letting them know he was all right. A nearby flight of steps led downward and Mike moved over to descend them. "You guys see Plummer? Where'd he go?"

Before Spence or Ben could yell a warning, Plummer emerged from behind a screen of boards at the landing directly below Mike. "I'm right here, Mike," he chuckled, stepping toward the boy.

Mike's hand rested on a sheet of rusty corrugated metal that wobbled under his touch. With the strength of desperation he pulled sharply on the panel and it broke free. Mike slammed it in front of Plummer's path, giving Mike time to whirl about and run up another conveyor belt.

This ramp led to the top of another platform, this time with neither ladder nor cable to offer a descent. The platform just stopped on the brink of a sixty-foot drop. Mike swung quickly around and found himself face-to-face with Plummer.

"Better not come any closer," the boy warned. "This plank won't hold both of us!"

The adult stepped forward anyway and rocked against the timbers that supported the end of the catwalk. He was grinning with sinister pleasure at his victory. "I don't think it's gonna hold one of us, buddy boy," he quipped. He kicked sharply at one of the supports, which broke free and fell. Mike's end of the platform sagged, and the boy hastily grabbed the other side to keep from falling.

"Hey!" Mike yelled.

Plummer idly bounced up and down, making the walk shimmy and sway. "Tell you the truth," he said, "I was getting kind of tired of chasing you anyway." With that the man kicked out the other support.

The boards under Mike's feet snapped!

Mike made a frantic grab for a bit of a rubber belt hanging from the edge of the precipice and managed to catch the last six inches of slack. He hung there dangling, his feet kicking futilely. He couldn't pull himself back up!

Testing his footing carefully, Plummer stepped closer to where Mike hung. "Doesn't look too good, Mike," he said cheerfully. "Hand up my keys, and I'll pull you up."

Swinging in a dizzying circle, Mike gulped and looked down. A tank half full of green scum was too far away; no escape that way. He saw Ben and

Spence crouched at the bottom of the conveyor incline, but what could they do?

"Still not gonna hand 'em over?" Plummer growled. "You're a stubborn boy, Mike. All right, let's make this a bit more interesting." He opened a pocketknife and began to saw through Mike's lifeline.

Ben and Spence had crept up behind Dan Plummer. They were only a dozen feet away. Spence handed something small and shiny to Ben, then gave the larger boy a length of pipe. With a crash, Ben jumped out and landed on the level just behind Plummer. He took a deep breath and raised the end of the pipe to his lips. With a fierce puff of air, he propelled the tranquilizer dart into the man's backside.

Plummer jolted upright, reaching back at the sudden sting and pulling out the dart. "Oh, you're gonna pay for that!" he growled at Ben.

Ben pivoted to run, tripped over the valve of a water pipe, and sprawled on the walkway. He rolled over, calling, "No, no!"

Extending his hands as if to grasp Ben around the neck and strangle the boy, Plummer advanced a step. The man swayed once and rubbed his hand across his eyes before continuing his attack.

"I'm dead," Ben mumbled. "Dead!"

Leaning forward toward Ben, Plummer staggered,

and his eyes suddenly rolled back in his head. Wobbling sideways, he put out a hand to steady himself and leaned heavily on a thin railing. It shattered with his weight. The man pitched outward, away from the steel frame, and fell headfirst into the vat of evil-looking liquid.

🌵

Though openmouthed with shock at Plummer's plunge through the railing, Spence and Ben wasted no time in rescuing Mike. They carefully pulled up the frayed belt until Mike's head appeared over the edge of the plank walkway. Then Ben reached under Mike's armpits and, giving a tremendous heave upwards, hauled his friend to safety.

"Man, am I glad to see you guys!" Mike sighed.

As the three started back to the ground, they paused to look at Plummer. Though saved from death by his dive into the tank, all the fight was gone out of him. Mike's attacker lay half-in and half-out of the shallow pool. One of his arms was draped over the rim, and he appeared barely able to keep himself from sliding back down in the ooze.

"We need to call for help for Smitty and for . . ." Mike gestured downward.

"Winnie's already taking care of that," Spence pointed out as he waved toward Smitty's truck.

The Navajo girl had reconnected the microphone and was sending out the call for assistance.

Help was not long in arriving either. Mike's grandfather, a deputy sheriff, an ambulance with two paramedics, and the veterinarian, Dr. Mangus, in his field-services truck, all rolled up within five minutes of each other.

Plummer was dragged from the tank, secured to a gurney, and loaded into the back of the ambulance. Smitty, coming around at last, was attended to by one of the emergency medical technicians, who bandaged the officer's head. The sheriff was declared to have just a minor wound— though, the paramedic chuckled, it was only due to Smitty's unbelievably hard head.

Dr. Mangus attended to the gorilla. With the help of the deputy and the kids, he loaded it into a cage on the back of his vehicle for transport to the animal clinic. The animal, revived from the drug, sat looking around with interest at the groups of people scurrying around. It did not seem to be unhappy at being back in the safety of a cage after its ordeal in the desert.

As things were getting sorted out, Ben approached Sheriff Smitty, toting a metal box. "Here it is," Ben said. "Out of Plummer's car."

Pop, looking on at the horde of precious metal, declared, "No question; it's gold."

Smitty gingerly felt the knot on the back of his head and said, "Plummer must have been trailing the gorilla when he came across Silas's deserted shack. He found the gold and saw an opportunity to—"

"Liberate it," Mike said, embarrassed that he had ever been ready to believe Plummer.

"Yep," Smitty agreed. "Just a common thief. He's no protector of animals either. Arlene ran his ID through the police computer. Turns out he's got a long record as a poacher. Probably planned to sell our friend's body parts overseas."

"Oh, no!" Ben fumed. "But he's OK, right, Dr. Mangus?"

"What are you going to do with him, Doc?" Mike asked.

"Get him out of this cage, into more suitable surroundings. He'll be fine," the vet assured the kids. "The folks at the reptile farm have agreed to put him up in a suitable pen until we track down the rightful owner. Who knows, maybe there's even a reward."

Ben slipped a final candy bar between the bars of the cage as Dr. Mangus started the truck. "Here ya go, boy," he said to his hairy friend. "One more for the road." The ape grunted his appreciation and almost seemed to smile.

As the vet's truck drove away, Pop walked up

and put his arm around Mike's shoulder. "Well, it looks like you kids have wrapped up another case," he said.

"Almost," Mike agreed. "Almost."

11

Silas Varner looked around at the noise made by four humming quad runners motoring up his gravel-covered drive. He stopped hammering a nail into the loose frame on the doorway he was repairing and waited.

He watched as the four Last Chance Detectives pulled up their vehicles and shut off the engines. While the other three kids remained outside,

Mike took Jake from the luggage rack and led him on a leash into the yard. "Mr. Varner," the boy said quietly.

"Fowler," the old prospector muttered. Then, slipping off his work gloves and advancing to meet Mike in the yard, the desert rat continued, "Guess I shouldn't be so quick to run you off my land this time. Smitty just left. He told me how you were responsible for getting my gold back. . . . Thanks."

Relieved that this was going better than he had feared, Mike said, "You're welcome, sir." Then he passed Jake's leash across to the man and added, "And here's the rest of what belongs to you. I apologize for taking Jake like I did. I realize now that it wasn't right."

"Apology accepted," Varner said, scratching the white stubble of his chin.

"He's gotten real used to eating every day, and—"

"I *know* how to keep him," Silas interrupted gruffly.

"Yeah," Mike agreed with resignation. The boy knelt beside the dog. "Bye, Jake," he said, ruffling the animal's fur. "You be good. . . . I'll never forget you."

The leader of the Last Chance Detectives turned to leave. His quick about-face let him see Winnie brushing away a tear, but no one else noticed. Then just as Mike mounted his quad, there was a frantic barking, and Jake bounced up alongside, putting his paws on the gas tank. "No, Jake," Mike scolded. "You gotta stay here with Mr. Varner."

Then Mike noticed that Jake was no longer wearing the leash that had been attached to his collar. The boy looked toward Silas for an explanation. Was it possible? Was that really the thin line of a smile stretching across the prospector's face? "Remember," Varner instructed with mock sternness, "he's got used to eatin' every day."

A wave of confusion and hope broke over Mike and the others. "You mean . . ."

"Now, go on," the miner demanded. "Better get out of here before I change my mind."

"Yeah!" Ben exulted.

"All right, Jake!" Winnie shouted.

"Thanks, Mr. Varner," Mike said. "Thanks . . . thanks a lot."

The old desert rat nodded slowly, then added, "Maybe ol' Jake can help you track down your dad someday."

Mike beamed. "I *bet* he can!" he exclaimed.

The gang strapped on their helmets and revved up their engines in triumph. They rode away, Jake running and barking excitedly after them. An enormous grin covered the features of the old prospector, who watched until they were completely out of sight.